MW00489137

ONLY HARD PROBLEMS

PROBLEMS

◄— A GALACTIC BONDS BOOK —►

JENNIFER ESTEP

ONLY HARD PROBLEMS
Copyright © 2024 by Jennifer Estep

*To all the readers who wanted more
Galactic Bonds books—this one is for you.*

To my mom—for everything.

*To characters like Zane Zimmer—who turn
out to be so much more than just villains.*

*To myself—for trying something different
and writing a book of my heart.*

.

The only certainty in the galaxy is that life brings only hard problems along with it.

—*AUTHOR UNKNOWN*

ONE

ZANE

The words haunted me.

Five little words, seven simple syllables, twenty-three ordinary letters.

And yet the combination of those words, syllables, and letters had rocked my perspective of, well, *everything*.

Everything I had always been told. Everything I had always believed. Everything I had always known to be an absolute *truth*—especially when it came to my family.

Vesper Quill is your sister.

Ah, those five pesky little words.

Kyrion Caldaren had telepathically whispered that thought to me while I had been escorting him to Lord Callus Holloway, the ruler of the Imperium, during a midnight ball at Crownpoint palace. Even now, two weeks later, I could still see the satisfied smirk on Kyrion's face as he tossed out the revelation like it was the ultimate trump card in the cutthroat Regal game we'd been playing our entire lives. Even worse, I could still feel his bloody *smugness* with my telempathy, like he was standing right beside me and grinding his stormsword into my ribs one slow, painful inch at a time—

"Lord Zane?" A low voice intruded on my dark thoughts. "Is the solstice suit not to your liking? You haven't said anything in five minutes."

A seventy-something man hovered by my side and studied me in the floor-length mirror propped up in the corner. He was a few inches shorter than me, with iron-gray hair, tan skin, and long, slender, nimble fingers that could wield a needle and thread with expert precision. Fergus had been the House Zimmer tailor longer than I had been alive.

Fergus's dark brown eyes flicked over me from top to bottom as he searched for faults in his work. "Per your instructions, I made the solstice suit a sleeker, more fashionable version of your Arrow uniform."

A crisp white shirt peeked out from the V at the top of the fitted tailcoat that stretched across my broad shoulders. The front of the coat only came down to my waist, although the twin tails in the back dropped to my knees. Two rows of blue opal buttons marched down the front of the ice-blue coat, while matching blue pants and knee-high black boots completed my ensemble. I almost always wore my family's colors, even though everyone already knew exactly who I was, thanks to the gossipcasts that breathlessly covered my exploits.

Fergus was wearing a similar tailcoat, although his was dark gray with ice-blue trim and silver buttons stamped with tiny Zs, a sign that he belonged to House Zimmer.

"How is it that you can make the same coat look dashing and distinguished, whereas I always feel like a little boy playing dress-up?" I grumbled.

A wry smile curved the corner of Fergus's mouth. "Skill, my lord." He gestured at my tailcoat in the mirror. "Although as you've told me many, many times, the ice blue of House Zimmer brings out your eyes much better than it does mine."

I studied my own reflection in the mirror. He was right. The ice-blue fabric did bring out the similar shade of my eyes. My grandmother and my father both had the same color eyes. So did several of my cousins. In fact, just about everyone with even a drop of Zimmer blood had ice-blue eyes.

Except for my sister.

Vesper had the dark blue eyes of her mother, Nerezza Blackwell, although silver flecks often appeared in Vesper's gaze whenever she was emotional, using her seer power, or tapping into her truebond connection with Kyrion—like she had during the midnight ball.

The memories erupted in my mind, as sharp, bright, and clear as videos playing on a holoscreen. Vesper and Kyrion in the middle of the throne room floor, yelling and crawling toward each other, even as Imperium soldiers tried to drag them away from each other . . . The two of them lunging toward each other, blue sparks flickering around their fingertips like tiny butterflies . . . The couple finally clasping hands, and those blue butterfly sparks coalescing and erupting into bright, crackling lightning that had danced around them in jagged forks as though they were caught in the center of a violent electrical storm . . .

"Zane?" Fergus asked in a low, hesitant voice. "Is something wrong?"

I blinked and focused on Fergus, who stared back at me, concern furrowing his forehead. The tailor was a true friend, and I had confided many things to him over the years, but I wasn't about to confess my inner turmoil. Not now. Not until I decided how I felt about having a long-lost sister—and all the tough truths and hard problems that came along with the startling revelation.

"Your design and work are impeccable as always, Fergus," I replied, forcing some false cheer into my voice.

He opened his mouth to ask another question, but I cut him

off and spewed out the first lie that popped into my head. "I was just thinking about the solstice celebration."

The summer solstice was the first major holiday and event since the disastrous midnight ball, and everyone who was anyone in Regal society was scheduled to attend. Except for Callus Holloway, of course. He rarely left the security of Crownpoint for any reason, preferring to force the Regals to come to the Imperium palace to seek an audience with him. But these days, the greedy siphon had a singular focus: finding Vesper and Kyrion so he could take the psionic power of their truebond connection for his own.

More memories crashed over me. Vesper and Kyrion battling Adria and Dargan Byrne, a pair of siblings who also had a truebond . . . A wounded Kyrion staring at me from the back of the open cargo bay while Vesper steered his blitzer, the *Dream World*, out of the Crownpoint docking bay . . . The spaceship streaking through the sky like a shooting star, carrying the couple to safety, before winking out of sight . . .

I blinked again. This time, I managed to banish the memories to the back of my brain, although annoyance sparked in my chest at the gigantic bloody *mess* Kyrion and Vesper had left behind—a mess that *I* was tasked with cleaning up. The true-bonded couple might have escaped Holloway's clutches, but in doing so, they had caused a multitude of problems for me.

Holloway had offered an enormous bounty for Kyrion and Vesper's capture, but no one had seen them since they had fled Corios, the planet that was the Imperium's seat of power.

There was a slight chance the couple was dead. A flight director had reported seeing Adria Byrne slip onto Kyrion's ship before it had left the Crownpoint docking bay. She could have killed Kyrion and Vesper in retaliation for her brother Dargan's death, but if so, she would have returned to Corios with their bodies. Adria's continued absence led me to believe that Kyrion and Vesper had ended her instead.

Holloway also thought they were still alive, which was the only thing we agreed on. He would probably spend the solstice holiday poring over supposed sightings of Kyrion and Vesper and listening to his generals theorize about where the couple might be heading. Arrogant fool. He should be worrying about what the Techwave was plotting next. The terrorist group was much more of a threat to the Imperium than Kyrion and Vesper, but Holloway always put his own dark desires and unending lust for power above everything else, including the people he was supposed to lead and protect.

"The solstice, eh?" Fergus said, drawing my attention back to him. A teasing grin spread across his face. "Wondering how many times you'll have to dance with Lady Asterin at the solstice ball to placate your grandmother?"

I bit back a groan. Lady Asterin Armas was yet another one of my many problems. "Something like that," I muttered.

Fergus reached up and clapped me on the shoulder. "Ah, don't look so dour. Asterin seems like a lovely woman. Dancing with her shouldn't be a chore. Besides, it's nothing you haven't done for the gossipcasts before, right?"

"Right," I replied, giving him a bright, cheerful smile in hopes of ending this unwanted topic of conversation.

Fergus's dark eyes narrowed. My patented smile might dazzle the gossipcast reporters, but he'd known me too long to be so easily fooled. Fergus hesitated, then squared his shoulders, as if bracing himself for an unpleasant task. "I've noticed some . . . tension between Beatrice and Wendell lately."

I dropped my gaze from his and tugged down my right sleeve, even though it was already perfectly in place. "What sort of tension?"

"Wendell seems to be greatly upset with your grandmother for some reason. Of course, I've asked Beatrice about it, but she said it was a minor squabble. Some new design that your father is having an issue with that she doesn't approve of."

I tugged down my left sleeve with a sharp motion, almost ripping off an opal cufflink. "You know how cranky my father gets when he's stuck on a project, and how much crankier my grandmother can be when she doesn't immediately see the results she wants. I'm sure they'll both figure it out soon, and then things will return to normal."

The lies dripped easily off my tongue, although guilt knotted my stomach. Fergus was a dear friend, and I hated deceiving him, but it was a necessary evil, like so many other things in my life, both as an Imperium Arrow and as the heir to House Zimmer.

I raised my gaze back to Fergus's and gave him another false smile. This one must have been much more convincing than the last, because some of the tension and worry eased out of his wrinkled face.

"Good to know," Fergus replied.

He smiled back at me, then gathered up his pins, scissors, spools of thread, rolls of fabric, and other supplies. Unlike many Regal tailors, Fergus eschewed magnetic and robotic technology in favor of simple, old-fashioned tools. His designs, like my beautiful tailcoat, often took hundreds of hours to complete, but the fit, stitching, and other details were exquisite and well worth the wait.

Fergus packed everything into a battered wooden sewing box, which he hoisted into the crook of his elbow. "See you at the ball, Zane."

"I wouldn't miss it, especially when I look this good." I winked at him, then spun around, making the tailcoat flap against my legs.

Fergus chuckled, then left the room.

As soon as the door shut behind him, the smile dropped from my face faster than a meteor plummeting toward the ground. I stepped down off the raised dais, moved away from the mirror, and wound my way past the tables, chairs, and settees piled high with books, weapons, plastipapers, and wayward tea mugs that filled my tower library. The housekeepers always clucked their tongues about the mess, but I found the clutter comforting—and I needed all the comfort I could get right now.

I went past a long table covered with chrome appliances, including a brewmaker and a beverage chiller, both designed by Vesper, and stopped in front of one of the windows. In the distance, catty-corner across a busy thoroughfare, Imperium soldiers were stationed in front of Castle Caldaren, an enormous, hulking, dark blue stone structure that looked as grim and dour as its absentee owner.

The soldiers had been guarding the castle for two weeks, more than long enough to know that Kyrion wasn't coming back anytime soon, and they shot bored looks at the horse-drawn carriages that rattled over the Boulevard, the wide cobblestone avenue that fronted many of the Regal homes, including my tower in Castle Zimmer. Several more Imperium soldiers were stationed nearby at the edge of Promenade Park, their bloodred uniforms and silver blasters making them resemble man-size flowers with metallic thorns that had sprouted out of the park's grassy, rolling lawns.

My tablet chimed. Time to finish getting ready for the solstice celebration.

I turned away from the window and went over to a nearby table. A small weapon that was a cross between a hairpin and a dagger rested atop an uneven stack of paper books. Blue opals and sapphsidian chips adorned the butterfly-shaped hilt, although dried blood crusted the thin, sharp silver blade, marring the weapon's delicate beauty. I'd been so busy chasing down leads for Holloway about where Kyrion and Vesper might have gone that I hadn't had a chance to clean Dargan Byrne's blood off the blade yet.

More memories drifted through my mind. Taking the

weapon from my mother's jewelry collection before the midnight ball . . . Handing the butterfly dagger over to Inga, one of the Crownpoint servants, so she could secretly slip it to Vesper . . . Vesper yanking the butterfly dagger out of her hair, whipping around, and stabbing Dargan with the blade . . .

For the third time, I blinked and pushed the memories away. I hadn't known about my familial connection to Vesper when I'd arranged for her to receive the dagger. I'd just wanted to ease my own guilty conscience and give her a sporting chance to escape the horrific fate Holloway had in mind for her. Without risking myself, of course.

But now . . . now I wondered if my subconscious had known the truth about Vesper all along.

I was a psion, a broad term that also included seers, siphons, spelltechs, and other people with telekinesis, telepathy, telempathy, and other extraordinary mental abilities. No one knew exactly where psionic powers came from or how to consistently replicate them with science and technology, which was why many folks referred to such abilities as magic. I was a particularly strong telekinetic, able to move objects with my mind, but perhaps something else in my psionic powers had whispered a warning and prompted me to act so recklessly. Either way, Vesper Quill had caused nothing but trouble ever since she'd burst into my life a few months ago.

I glared down at the sparkling jewels, then reached past the dagger and grabbed my stormsword off an even larger and more haphazard pile of books. The long, sharp blade was made of lunarium, a precious mineral that enhanced psionic abilities and could even transform them into physical elements like fire, ice, lightning, and wind. The opalescent blade gleamed with a pale blue sheen in a reflection of my own psion power, but the bits of sapphsidian embedded in the silver hilt seemed to soak up the late-afternoon sunlight, making the jewels look black rather than the deep blue they truly were.

I traced my index finger over a piece of sapphsidian nestled in among the many Zs that were carved into the hilt. Perhaps it was my imagination, but the jewel looked like a wide, open, accusing eye embedded in the silver, like Vesper Quill herself was staring at me from somewhere deep inside my own sword. She was a seer. It wasn't out of the realm of possibility that she could be psionically spying on me.

Vesper seemed to be quite powerful in her own right, and her truebond with Kyrion would make her even stronger, since the connection would allow the two of them to share thoughts, feelings, and instincts, along with strength, fighting skills, and psionic abilities. During the midnight ball, their combined psion power had ripped through the Crownpoint throne room in a vicious shock wave, toppling bronze sculptures off the walls, cracking the white marble floor, and knocking over Regals, servants, and guards. Vesper peering at me through a jewel in my own sword would be child's play compared with that previous decimation. Or perhaps it was just my own turbulent thoughts giving life to such fanciful musings.

I had always been so bloody *proud* that my sword bore the Zimmer family sigil, just as I had always been so proud to wear the ice-blue color of House Zimmer. But now . . . now I didn't know how I felt about my family tree, especially this new, unexpected branch.

Holloway might be focused on where Vesper and Kyrion were going, but ever since they had fled from Corios, I had been secretly retracing their steps, trying to learn everything I could about my wayward sister and the rogue Arrow who had been my former boss.

I didn't have all the details, but someone—most likely Daichi Hirano, Kyrion's chief of staff—had discreetly hacked into the Regal archives a few months ago to compare various DNA samples. Daichi had hidden his tracks well but not quite well enough. According to the time stamps I'd found, Daichi—and by extension Kyrion—had been trying to figure out who Vesper's father was for months, although they hadn't matched my DNA to Vesper's until *after* the midnight ball.

I had no idea how Kyrion had figured out that Vesper was my sister without the DNA confirmation. Perhaps I would ask the smug bastard when I finally caught up with him.

But the more important question was: What did *Vesper* think about the information? That she was a Zimmer? That Wendell was her father? That *I* was her brother?

Most people would have been absolutely *thrilled*, especially since House Zimmer was among the most powerful Regal Houses, with an abundance of wealth and influence. At the very least, Vesper could have engineered a hefty payday out of the information. Many Regal lords and ladies were known for having ill-advised dalliances, especially when they were away from their home planet of Corios, and it was quite common for Regals to pay off unwanted children to disappear back to the tourist planets and other distant reaches of the galaxy from whence they came.

But so far, there had been no communication from Vesper. No demands for money, no threats to sell the scandalous story to the gossipcasts, no dire warnings about all the ways she was going to torture us with the information.

The silence worried me. I didn't know Vesper Quill very well, but she was smart, strong, and more than capable of causing immense financial pain to House Zimmer and severe emotional trauma to my family. More so than she had already caused by simply existing.

My tablet chimed again, a little louder and sharper. I sighed. Like a prince out of an old-fashioned fairy tale, it was time for me to attend the ball, whether I wanted to or not.

So I shoved my stormsword into a slot on my belt and stomped out of the library, secrets and schemes still swirling around in my mind.

I went downstairs, knocked on an open door, and stepped into the enormous library that was my grandmother's domain, and thus the heart of Castle Zimmer.

Beatrice's library was easily five times the size of my own cozy, cluttered tower and was far more ostentatious, with polished wooden tables, glittering jeweled knickknacks, and delicate, spindly chairs and settees covered with velvet cushions and plump pillows. The area was absolutely immaculate, with everything in its place and a place for everything, from the perfectly aligned books on the shelves to the fresh blue-moon peonies standing tall in their vases to the three separate tea sets arranged on three separate tables, complete with serving platters, silverware, napkins, and delicate porcelain bowls brimming with Z-shaped sugar cubes.

Even my grandmother's desk was spotless, with a fresh pad of ice-blue paper, a pot of dark blue ink, and an old-fashioned crystal ink pen resting on a white lace doily. Seeing the House Zimmer colors on her desk further soured my mood.

My father, Wendell Zimmer, was already in the library, standing in front of a large silver-framed painting that hung between two bookcases. In the portrait, my father beamed at my mother, Miriol, who beamed right back at him. My mother had been quite lovely, with light brown hair and eyes and pale skin, although I had my father's blond hair, tan skin, and the ubiquitous blue eyes of House Zimmer.

Miriol had died of a sudden illness a few months after I'd been born, so I had never known her. Even now, thirty-eight years after her death, my father didn't talk about her much, as though simply saying her name was still too painful.

"Your mother always loved the solstice celebrations," Wendell said in a low, wistful voice when I stopped beside him.

"That's how we met. At a summer solstice celebration. Miriol had flowers and ribbons in her hair, and she was dancing with her friends like she was a fairy goddess come to life. She was the most beautiful thing I'd ever seen. I desperately wanted to talk to her, but I was so nervous and awkward that I couldn't make myself approach her. I was still working up my nerve when . . ."

". . . when she danced right up to you, gave you a crown of braided flowers, grabbed your hand, and pulled you along with her. Naturally, you fell in love with her right on the spot." I finished his thought in a gentle voice.

A faint smile flickered across his face. "I might have told you this story before."

"Just a few dozen times," I said, keeping my voice light.

Father smiled again, but the expression quickly wilted. "But I've never told you much about what happened after your mother died. How . . . distraught I was. How I . . . lashed out at the galaxy at large. How I made some . . . foolish choices, especially when it came to the company I kept."

Wendell looked up at the portrait again, but his eyes were dark and distant, as though he was peering back into his troubled past.

I tensed. He had to be talking about Nerezza Blackwell, Vesper's mother. I'd made some discreet inquiries and had my spies and other contacts dig up all the dirt they could find on Nerezza. As a teenager, she had been a poor nobody from a Temperate planet, but the Regals were always looking for psionic outliers to bolster their numbers and bloodlines, and Nerezza had had enough power and potential to be invited to attend a prestigious academy here on Corios. Somehow her path had crossed with my father's, and Vesper had been the result.

"What sort of company do you mean?" I asked in a careful voice.

Father opened his mouth, then stopped and cleared his throat, as though he wanted to tell me something important but wasn't quite sure how to phrase it.

How *did* one reveal he had a daughter he'd never known about? Even among the Regals, with all their archaic societal rules, there was no procedure for such a thing. For once, even my grandmother, with all her conniving, didn't have a Regal rule book she could follow, no accepted or proper or patented method to break the shocking news. Or perhaps she was determined to keep me in the dark along with everyone else, to quietly sweep aside this untidiness with Vesper the same way the servants removed the smallest specks of dust from her library. Hard to tell. Beatrice was always playing her own games, even within our family.

Either way, neither my father nor my grandmother had revealed that I'd gone from an only child to a big brother overnight. At first, I thought they had been as stunned as I had been, but as the days had gone by with no confession from either one of them, and not so much as the smallest bloody *hint* that anything had changed, their silence had begun to anger me.

"What do you want to tell me, Father?" I asked, my voice rougher and more insistent than before. "Just go ahead and say it. Whatever it is, I will understand. I promise."

Especially since I already knew his deep, dark secret, but I was determined to be as kind as possible. My father might be second-in-command of House Zimmer, but he wasn't brash and ruthless like me and my grandmother. Wendell was a kind, gentle, sensitive soul, and he would have been quite happy to spend the rest of his life puttering around in his workshop rather than dueling with the other lords and ladies in Regal society.

Father looked me in the eyes, sucked in a breath, and opened his mouth—

"Sorry I'm late," a familiar voice called out. "I had to make sure our gift had arrived."

Heels clacked against the stone floor in a high, sharp drumbeat. My father flinched and snapped his lips shut.

Beatrice Zimmer, my grandmother, swept inside the library with all the grace and elegance of a queen, and her long ice-blue gown swished around her legs like a bell swinging back and forth, softly announcing her arrival. Her silver hair was piled on top of her head, and blue opals glinted among the curls like a hidden crown. Her skin was more rosy than tan, but her eyes were the same ice-blue as my father's—and just as cold and calculating as mine.

Beatrice's gaze zipped between my father and me before shooting up to my mother's portrait on the wall. She raised one eyebrow in a chiding motion at my father, who glared right back at her. I didn't have all the details, but from what I'd overheard, Beatrice had kept Vesper's existence a secret from my father, something Wendell was furious about. Most of the Regals might shun their bastard children, but my father was too softhearted to ever do anything that cruel. If he'd known about Vesper, he would have immediately welcomed her into our home, scandal be damned, and doted on her as much as he had always doted on me.

Beatrice stared at my father. When it became apparent that he was going to keep quiet, she strode over and thrust a box into my hands. Delicate silver filigree ribboned across the pale, opalescent lunarium in elegant whorls and scrolls. Not just any box but a jewelry box.

My gut twisted with dread, but I cracked open the top to reveal a wide silver choker studded with large blue opals. Even by Regal standards, it was an impressive, expensive piece, and I let out a low, appreciative whistle.

"Aw, Grandmother, you shouldn't have," I drawled. "Although it will look absolutely *marvelous* with my new tailcoat."

Beatrice rolled her eyes. "It's for Lady Asterin. A summer solstice gift from you is appropriate at this stage of your courtship."

I rolled my eyes right back at her. "This is not a mere *gift*. Why, there are enough jewels on this thing to feed everyone in the city for at least a month. Two months, if you only dish out porridge and gruel."

My grandmother rolled her eyes again. "Your exaggerations are excessive, as always. No one serves gruel anymore."

"Why are you so determined to snare Asterin? I've told you numerous times that she openly despises me. I feel the exact same way about her, although I, of course, am too much of a gentleman to let such animosity show." I finished my thought with a haughty harrumph of disapproval.

My father snorted in disbelief. I winked at him, which only made him snort again, this time with laughter.

Beatrice ignored us both and jutted out her chin in a defiant look I knew all too well. "Asterin might despise you, and you might loathe her, but her family greatly admires the House Zimmer name, fortune, and connections, especially now that you are the head of the Arrows, as you should have been all along."

Her chin jutted out even more. "Besides, you know I have a sense about these things. You and Asterin will make a lovely couple."

I groaned. Beatrice was a very powerful telempath who could easily sense other people's emotions, even over great distances. Every once in a while, she would also have a vision of the future, just like I sometimes did. But worst of all, she considered herself a bloody *matchmaker*, claiming that her strong telempathy gave her insight about which lords and ladies would be perfect for each other.

Beatrice had crowed so loudly and consistently about her supposed *gift* that some of the other Regals now came to her for advice when they were trying to marry off their relatives. But it was all simply another sly scheme on my grandmother's part, a way for her to subtly push certain Regals together and form alliances that would ultimately benefit House Zimmer in some way.

"You should listen to your grandmother," Wendell chimed in. "After all, she *always* knows what's best for our family, even when we don't know ourselves. Isn't that right, Beatrice?"

She bristled at his snide tone. My father only called her Beatrice when he was upset with her, something neither one of them thought I noticed. They glared at each other again, and the air crackled with so much tension that I would probably get a violent static shock if I brushed up against either one of them.

"Oh, yes, family *is* the most important thing. Family first, then House Zimmer, then the galaxy can take care of everyone else," I drawled again. "Isn't that what you always say, Grandmother?"

Beatrice's eyes narrowed, the wheels clearly spinning in her mind as she tried to figure out what—if anything—I knew about Vesper. I gave her the same dazzling smile that I always gave the gossipcast reporters.

She arched an eyebrow at me in the same chiding motion she'd used on Father earlier. Like Fergus, my grandmother was not so easily fooled.

"Come," Beatrice said, smoothing her hands down her skirt. "The carriage is waiting. We don't want to be late."

"Oh, no," my father said, his voice still snide and bitter. "We wouldn't want to appear to be anything but the perfect Regal family we are."

He glared at her again, then stormed out of the library. Beatrice watched him go, her lips pinching together into a tight line.

"Father has been upset with you for weeks now. Anything

you want to tell me?" I asked, hoping she would finally just admit what was going on.

Beatrice's lips parted, and she drew in a breath. Then she shook her head, and her breath escaped in a soft sigh. "Nothing for you to worry about, my darling. Just an old problem that has reared its ugly head yet again, despite my best efforts to contain it. Don't fret. I'm sure everything will work itself out for the best."

She nodded at the jewelry box in my hand. "Make sure to give the necklace to Asterin during the celebration."

Beatrice hesitated, then stepped forward, reached up, and patted my cheek, her fingers warm and firm against my skin. "I've always done what I think is best for our family, and the best is all that I've ever wanted for you and your father. I want you to know that, Zane."

"Of course," I murmured.

Beatrice patted my cheek again, then left the library.

I rolled my tense shoulders and shut the necklace box. The sharp *snap* of the lid closing rang out as loudly as a Frozon bear trap clamping around my ankle. Despite all my protests to the contrary, my grandmother was still determined to shackle me to Asterin. I wasn't a seer like Vesper, but for some strange reason, I felt like the trap had already been sprung, and all I could do was snarl and flail helplessly in its tight teeth.

Perhaps I was wrong. Perhaps the solstice celebration would go better than the midnight ball had.

I bloody hoped so—for all our sakes.

TWO

ZANE

I tucked the lunarium jewelry box into my pocket. I adjusted my tailcoat, but the square box was as heavy as a blaster pressing against my heart. I muttered a curse, then left the library, went out the front door, and stepped into the waiting carriage. It too was ice-blue, inside and out, and the enormous round passenger compartment always made me feel like I'd been swallowed alive by an oversize satin pumpkin.

My grandmother was sitting in one side of the carriage, staring out the window, while my father was in the opposite corner, watching a gossipcast on his tablet. Once again, the space between them crackled with tension. I bit back a sigh, slid in next to my father, and thumped my fist on the low ceiling. A second later, the horses plodded forward, and the carriage creaked along the cobblestones.

Dozens of other carriages were also rolling along the Boulevard, right past Promenade Park. Hundreds of people were already picnicking on the park's rolling lawns, enjoying games, music, and more in honor of the summer solstice, which was a city- and planet-wide holiday.

A few gossipcasters and their videographers had set up their cameras on the edge of the grass and were filming the Regals as we all left our castles for our own solstice celebration. I stuck my head out of the carriage window and waved, catching their attention.

"Woo-hoo! See you at the party!" I called out in a booming, grandiose voice, then added another *Woo-hoo!* for good measure.

Several of the gossipcasters—women and men alike—tittered and waved back at me. To them, I was a veritable Prince Charming with the perfect Regal life. Right now, I would have much rather been preening for the cameras than stuck in this carriage with my angry, secretive family.

The carriage quickly left the park behind and rolled past Crownpoint, the Imperium palace. Unlike the Regals' colorful castles with their quirky turrets and fanciful parapets that lined the Boulevard, the palace had a plain, ugly façade of chrome and glass, and its miles-high towers glinted like rows of spears in the bright afternoon sunlight.

My gaze locked on the main tower. Callus Holloway hadn't messaged me today. He probably thought his silence was punishment, but I welcomed the respite from his constant demands that I find Kyrion and Vesper and his not-so-subtle threats about what would happen to me, and my family, if I failed to deliver the truebonded couple to him—

Ding! The shrill tone I'd assigned to Holloway erupted from my tablet. No respite after all. I sighed, pulled the device out of my pocket, and read the message.

Quit preening for the gossipcasts like an idiot. Have some fucking dignity.

So Holloway was watching the solstice coverage and, therefore, me too. Terrific. On the bright side, he never expected replies, only obedience, so I shoved my tablet back into my pocket.

"Is there a problem?" my father asked in a worried voice.

I shrugged off his concern. "Just Holloway being Holloway. I'm clearly his new favorite. He messages me more than a lovestruck schoolboy."

My father smiled at my joke, but the expression quickly faded away. Beatrice eyed me a moment, then stared out the window again.

Forty-five minutes later, the carriage zipped through an open gate, entered a spaceport, and crisscrossed several long runways before rolling up the cargo-bay ramp of a massive transport. The driver stopped the carriage in the allotted House Zimmer spot nestled in the middle of dozens of other Regal carriages. Horses whinnied, and the murmuring of voices and the chiming of tablets trilled through the air like a muted symphony. A few Regals leaned out of their windows and gossiped with their neighbors, but everyone remained inside their carriages.

I thumped my head back against the cushion. Even for Regal society, this was grandiose overkill. It would have been so much simpler and easier for everyone to take mechanized transports to the celebration site, but alas, the horse-drawn carriage ride along the Boulevard was one of the summer solstice traditions, although I had no idea what it actually celebrated, other than the Regals' excessive wealth and obsession with opulence.

Once the horses were tended to and the carriages were locked in place, the thrusters fired up, and the transport lifted off the ground. Beatrice pulled out her tablet to watch the gossipcast coverage, while my father kept studying his device, both still ignoring each other.

I pulled out my own tablet and scrolled through my messages, checking in with all my contacts, as well as some of the other Arrows. Beatrice was an accomplished spy wrangler, with eyes and ears throughout Regal society and out into the galaxy beyond, but over the years, I had built my own network, which was useful for times like these when I wanted information without my grandmother getting wind of it.

Still no confirmed sightings of Vesper and Kyrion, but it was just a matter of time before someone spotted them, especially given the massive bounty Holloway had announced for their capture. I responded to a few messages and read the latest reports from Holloway's generals about where the couple might have gone, but no one had any concrete information or actionable intelligence.

I shut Vesper and Kyrion out of my mind and focused on another one of my many hard problems: tracking down the Techwave. Over the last several months, the terrorist group had attacked one Regal facility after another across the galaxy, killing workers and stealing all the weapons, tech, and resources they could carry away. But they had been surprisingly quiet in recent weeks, which made me uneasy. The Techwave was no doubt gearing up for another attack, although none of Holloway's spies had any clue when or where the Techies might strike next.

An hour later, the transport began its descent, and we all put away our tablets. Beatrice and Wendell hadn't spoken a word to each other the entire ride, and I saw no need to break the tense, angry silence. My grandmother had taught me that Zimmers always put on a happy face in public, and right before a major Regal celebration was no time to instigate family drama.

The transport touched down, the cargo-bay ramp descended, and the carriages were unlocked from their spots. Then the horses circled around and trotted down the ramp. Once again, we crisscrossed several spaceport runways before going through a wide, open gate. This time, instead of cobblestone streets and colorful castles, crushed-shell driveways and quaint cottages stretched out into the Corios countryside.

I stuck my head out the window again. The fresh scent of summer grass tickled my nose, along with the sharp tang of wild onions and the earthy aroma of mud from last night's heavy rains. Corios was a Temperate planet with four distinct seasons, and thunderstorms often popped up in the hot, humid summer months. Lightning had cracked several branches off the flowering trees, and white, purple, and yellow blossoms were scattered across the roadways like petals a girl had plucked out of a flower basket.

Thirty minutes later, a massive castle appeared in the distance. The wealthier and more prominent Regal families took turns hosting the winter and summer solstice celebrations. Today, Lord Jorge Rojillo of House Rojillo had that honor—and headache.

Castle Rojillo sprawled across the top of a grassy hill that overlooked a man-made lake surrounded by dense coniferous woods. The castle was made of a beautiful pale pink stone that made it gleam like a colorful diamond nestled in the surrounding green, blue, and brown landscape. Every level of the structure featured round windows, fluted columns, and scalloped archways that reminded me of the edges of a seashell. White flags boasting the large stylized, flowering pink *R* of House Rojillo fluttered atop the castle's many turrets, along with a lone limp flag bearing a bronze hand on a red background—Callus Holloway's sigil and a token nod to the Imperium leader.

The horses climbed the hill and stopped in front of the castle. I opened the door and hopped out, not wanting to spend a second longer inside the tension-filled carriage. My father also hopped out, and I helped my grandmother climb down. All around us, other Regals were also arriving, and their chatter droned through the air like a cloud of excited bees, accentuated by the steady *crunch-crunch-crunch-crunch* of the horses' hooves through the crushed shells underfoot.

One of my father's friends called out a greeting, and Wendell waved and headed in that direction without a backward glance.

My grandmother's lips pinched into a tight line again. After a few seconds, she smoothed out her expression and turned to me.

"Remember what we talked about," she said in a stern voice. "You will be charming and attentive to Lady Asterin at the ball. Then, when the time is right, you will present her with the solstice gift."

"Yes, yes, yes," I said, tapping my chest where the jewelry box was still nestled inside my coat pocket. "I'll make all the appropriate remarks about how the necklace is but a mere humble token of my deep affection and will only enhance her own beauty, which needs no adornments to begin with, given how innately glorious she already is."

Beatrice huffed. "I know you are not fond of Asterin, but her family has important connections, influence, and resources in the Erzton—things House Zimmer might very well need to survive the brewing war with the Techwave."

Unlike the Imperium, which focused on Regal bloodlines and psionic abilities, or the Techwave, with its rabid devotion to technology and horrific scientific experiments, the Erzton dealt in something much more solid and substantial: minerals, metals, and other raw materials needed to make everything from blasters to spaceships to the ridiculously ornate carriage we had just arrived in.

"What's wrong?" I asked in a sharp, suspicious voice. "What aren't you telling me?"

My grandmother gave an airy wave of her hand, making the jeweled rings on her fingers flash like warning lights on a crashing blitzer. "Nothing concrete, darling. Truly. My spies are reporting that the Techwave and our other enemies are quiet for the moment."

"But?"

"But our old, well-known enemies are usually only quiet right before they strike, and that is what worries me." Her words echoed my earlier thoughts, and her gaze cut to my father, who was still talking to his friends. "And then, of course, there are always new enemies we must be concerned about. As well as unexpected threats from within our own ranks."

Was that how my grandmother saw Vesper? As a new enemy? An unexpected threat that might prompt Wendell to turn against her, against House Zimmer?

Because that was not how I saw Vesper.

In the beginning, Vesper Quill had been a mere annoyance, a smartass engineer whose cleverness and doggedness had gotten her embroiled in Rowena Kent's treasonous plot against the Imperium. Once Vesper had become a Regal, she had been a potential adversary, especially given how cozy she and Kyrion had seemed at the ball held in her honor. Then Holloway had made Vesper a target by ordering me and Adria and Dargan Byrne to capture her. But now that she was a fugitive, now that I knew the truth about our connection . . . Well, Vesper was nothing but a giant problem—and I *hated* problems.

"Anyway, darling, I must mingle. We'll talk more later—*after* you give Asterin the solstice gift." Beatrice speared me with a pointed look, then glided away to speak to her own friends.

Slowly but surely, all the Regals were heading toward the enormous pink scalloped archway that served as the castle's main entrance. I tugged on my jacket sleeves, then plastered a sunny smile on my face and strode forward, waving and calling out greetings to everyone, friend and foe alike.

The white crushed-shell driveway narrowed into a wide path that was lined on one side with pink velvet ropes. Dozens of gossipcasters were standing in the cordoned-off section, stretching their microphones and cameras out as far as they could without toppling over the ropes. Many of the Regals ignored the gossipcasters, hurrying right on by them, but it was always better to make allies than enemies, especially with people who would beam my slightest social gaffe across the galaxy with ruthless glee. So I swaggered straight toward the cameras—straight into the heart of the fight—like I always did. The gossipcasters all perked up at the sight of me heading toward them. "Zane! Lord Zane! How are you feeling? Who are you wearing?"

The usual shouted questions washed over me, and I stopped, put one hand on the hilt of my stormsword, and lifted my chin, striking a haughty pose and letting the cameras soak me up in all my sun-dappled glory.

"I'm feeling marvelous! The summer solstice is one of my favorite celebrations of the social season. You all know that I'm always happy for any excuse to have a good time."

I gave an exaggerated wink, and several of the gossipcasters laughed. Zane Zimmer was nothing if not charming.

"I, of course, am wearing the fabulous design of Fergus, the exclusive House Zimmer tailor." I turned left and right, showing off my spiffy new tailcoat.

"Zane! Zane!" another gossipcaster called out. "What are your thoughts on your new shampoo commercial? Galactic Suds for Studs?"

Ah, the shampoo commercial. Three cringeworthy minutes of footage that showed me bare-chested and splashing around in an old-fashioned porcelain tub filled with bubbles, shampoo bottles, and rubber duckies, while I chirped about how clean, fresh, and tingly said shampoo made me feel. I'd shot the commercial a few months ago, and it had started airing the night of the disastrous midnight ball.

The shampoo itself was a wonderful, organic, responsibly sourced product, but the commercial was perhaps the most embarrassing one on my Regal résumé. Still, Galactic Suds had given me a delightful number of credits to hawk their brand, along with a lifetime supply of shampoo, and I was going to give the company their money's worth.

I raked a hand through my longish blond hair and looked

straight into the closest camera. "I'm having a magnificent time working with Galactic Suds for Studs. The name says it all, right?"

I gave another exaggerated wink. More laughter rang out, along with a few snide snickers, but it all washed right off me, just like the shampoo had in the shower earlier. I'd humiliated myself in the past far worse—and for far fewer credits than what Galactic Suds for Studs was paying me.

I strutted along the media line, speaking to one gossipcaster after another, along with all their camerapeople. Hands were shaken, questions were answered, more winks and compliments were doled out. I was almost to the end of the line when a gossipcaster with particularly long arms shoved her microphone forward. I had to jerk back to keep from getting bonked in the nose.

"Zane! Zane!" the gossipcaster called out. "How goes the hunt for Kyrion Caldaren and Vesper Quill?"

We were officially through with the easy, frivolous questions, and the usual gossipy sparring session had just morphed into a full-fledged media battle.

I ground my teeth and forced myself to smile even wider. "I'm hot on their trail. They can run, but they can't hide, especially not from Zane Zimmer."

A few laughs sounded, but far more snide snickers rang out this time, and several people rolled their eyes. My arrogant antics might be good for their ratings, but many of the gossipcasters found me as ridiculous as most of the Regals did. But that was okay. Ridiculous people were often underestimated, and I'd buried my sword in more than one enemy's gut because of their lack of judgment. My pretty face masked the heart of a moon-cold killer.

"What about the other Regals?" the pesky gossipcaster called out again. "Aren't you worried that they'll offer shelter and aid to Lord Kyrion?"

I barely restrained myself from rolling my own eyes. Kyrion Caldaren was an aloof, uptight, broody bastard. He didn't have any *friends* among the Regals, and the opportunistic lords and ladies would turn him in the second they got the chance to collect the bounty credits and ingratiate themselves with Holloway.

"Of course not," I replied in a smooth voice. "We all know the Regals' loyalty lies squarely with Callus Holloway and the Imperium, not with Kyrion Caldaren."

"Any news on Nerezza Blackwell?" The pesky gossipcaster just kept spewing out annoying, awkward questions. "What about your efforts to track her down?"

Once again, I ground my teeth to hold on to my smile. "Nerezza Blackwell remains a person of interest. She too will be brought back to Corios to face justice for her many crimes against the Imperium, including conspiring with the Techwave."

During the midnight ball, not only had Vesper revealed that Nerezza was her biological mother, but she'd also claimed that the Regal lady was a double agent, spying on both the Techwave *and* the Imperium to further her own mysterious agenda. During the chaos and confusion of the throne room fight, Nerezza had slipped out of Crownpoint, emptied out the House Blackwell accounts, and fled Corios in a private space cruiser.

No one had seen or heard from the Regal lady since then, although I knew that Beatrice was greatly worried about what Nerezza might do next—and what she might reveal about her relationship with Wendell, especially the fact that he was Vesper's father.

In addition to learning more about Vesper, I'd also been re-searching Nerezza. Even among the Regals, who put a capital *R* in Ruthless, Nerezza Blackwell was famous—or rather infamous—for being a notorious social climber who flitted from one relationship to another until she got what she wanted out of it.

Everything I'd discovered about her made my skin crawl. Story after story about Nerezza befriending, beguiling, and bewitching some lord, lady, servant, or guard, only to cast them aside the second they were no longer useful. Add in the fact that she'd done the same thing to her own daughter when Vesper was a child . . . Well, Nerezza Blackwell was far more devious, duplicitous, and dangerous than I'd imagined. She was another hard problem I didn't have a solution to, just like Vesper was.

The gossipcaster sucked in a breath to pepper me with yet more pointed questions, so I picked up my pace. "Sorry, folks. Gotta jet. Don't want to be late to the party. After all, there are several ladies who haven't had the pleasure of a dance with yours truly yet this social season."

I gave them all another exaggerated wink, along with a good-bye wave, then stepped through an archway into a large courtyard that featured a bubbling fountain. All the other Regals had already moved deeper into the castle, so I slid to the side, stopped in the shadows, and unscrewed the smile from my face.

Outside, the gossipcasters milled around, checking their equipment and footage and chatting with one another.

The woman who'd asked me about Kyrion, Vesper, and Nerezza lowered her microphone and shook her head. Her snide voice drifted over to me: "Zane Zimmer, always the arrogant idiot."

Her cameraman snickered in agreement. "How long do you think ol' Zane will last as the leader of the Arrows? I put down a hundred credits on one month—or less."

So there was a betting pool devoted to my expected failure and future execution. Fantastic.

The gossipcaster shrugged. "Depends on how quickly he

captures Kyrion Caldaren and Vesper Quill. But if he doesn't? Not long. Callus Holloway isn't known for his patience. Sooner or later, he'll order his Bronze Hand guards to chop Zane's empty, pretty head right off his pretty shoulders."

The cameraman snickered again, and the two of them started talking about other things. Their mocking dismissal didn't anger me, though. I'd worked long and hard to convince everyone that I was an arrogant idiot, just like they had said.

No, the thing that bothered me was they were right. If I didn't find my wayward sister soon, then my head would be the one on the chopping block.

I let myself brood for a minute, then plastered another smile on my face and stepped out of the shadows. I moved through the open-air courtyard, then two more similar areas, before finally reaching another scalloped archway that led to a massive lawn rolling out from the back of the castle like an emerald carpet.

Castle Rojillo was famous for its pink-star honeysuckles, which boasted blossoms bigger than my hand and perfumed the air with a sweet, delicate scent. Dozens of the dense green bushes ringed the lawn, starting at the castle walls and running all the way down to the man-made lake in the distance. The enormous, oversize bushes stretched up more than twenty feet, and strings of pink bulbs snaked through the tops of the thick branches, along with yellow and white crystals shaped like suns and crescent moons that cast rainbow prisms across the entire lawn.

Solstice games had been set up on one side of the grass, and children ran from one booth to another, smiling and shrieking while they tossed rings around toy planets, shot paint blasters at paper star charts, and smashed plastic models of space cruisers with wooden stormswords to spill out all the candy crammed inside. Other children clustered around the refreshment tables, using their bare hands to snag the colorful sugar bubbles that wafted up out of the dessert fountains and cram the sticky treats into their mouths.

Down at the lake, a few children splashed around in the shallows while parents and lifeguards watched from the relative dryness of a nearby dock. Farther out on the water, several Regals clutched frilly lace parasols and perched in the back of paddleboats being propelled by sweating servants. In the distance, beyond the far edge of the lake, the sun was beginning to set behind the surrounding hills and was streaking the sky in warm, hazy stripes of pink, orange, and yellow.

Summer solstice was the longest day of the year on Corios. It was just after eight, and the sun wouldn't fully vanish until almost nine o'clock galactic time. Eventually, the children would be put to bed inside the castle, while the adults waltzed around the dance floor that had been erected on the other side of the lawn. The ball would last into the wee hours of the morning, and many of the Regals would stumble to their rooms, high on chembonds and eager to indulge in all their fantasies—whether it was with their spouse, a servant, a guard, or some other convenient lover.

Ding! Another message from Holloway popped up on my tablet. *The only reason you're attending the solstice celebration is to see if any of the Regals are helping Kyrion. Don't forget that.*

As if I could with his charming missives. I huffed at his petty demands and slid my tablet back into my pocket.

A waving motion caught my eye, and I headed over to my father, who was standing near the refreshment tables with Jorge Rojillo, the head of House Rojillo.

"Hello, Zane!" Jorge called out, clapping me on the back.

I smiled at him, my expression genuine for a change. "Hello, Jorge."

Jorge Rojillo was in his early sixties, roughly the same age as my father, although he was much shorter, with a broad, stocky body. Like all the other Regal men in attendance, he was wearing a formal tailcoat, although his was the pale pink of House Rojillo and studded with flower-shaped gold buttons. Jorge plucked a white handkerchief out of his pocket, pushed back his wavy black hair, and dabbed some sweat off his bronze skin.

Tempered silk might adjust to the body heat of its wearer, along with the environment, but it was simply no match for the summer solstice sun. The hot rays beat down on my head, while the excessive humidity bathed everything in an unpleasant stickiness. Several lords and ladies were firmly ensconced in chairs in front of large box-shaped fans spaced around the lawn that were spewing out cooler air, as well as filtering out the worst of the summer pollen.

"Jorge was telling me about some new temperature-shielding technology he's been developing," my father said.

Jorge was a spelltech, someone who was capable of infusing psionic power into weapons and other objects, just like my father. And just like my father, Jorge preferred to spend most of his time in his research-and-development labs and left the Regal politicking up to his wife, Halecia, who was currently deep in conversation with Beatrice.

Jorge gave a modest shrug, although his dark brown eyes gleamed, and a satisfied grin spread across his face. "It's just a little something new I've whipped up. House Rojillo is bidding on the climate-control contracts for Promenade Park, and my latest invention should help put my proposal over the top."

The Regals liked to control everything, even the weather, when possible, which was why certain sections of Promenade Park were subject to strict climate control. The constant temperatures and set amounts of water, nutrients, and sunlight helped to ensure that many of the park's trees, bushes, and flowers bloomed all year round, instead of just in the spring.

"What does your new temperature-shielding technology do?" I asked in a polite voice, even as I inwardly groaned.

Jorge's face lit up the same way my father's face always did when he was talking about the latest gizmo he'd dreamed up. "Well, right now, the shielding is just a personal device. You strap it to your wrist, and it creates a bubble of air around your body that can be set to your preferred temperature no matter how hot or cold the ambient air is. It's like wearing your own thermostat. The shielding technology can also do other things, like filter out unwanted odors and repel flies, mosquitos, and other annoying insects. Here. Let me show you the prototype."

He slid his handkerchief back into his pocket, then pulled up his coat sleeve. A small device with a wide silver band, a small holoscreen, and glittering bits of lunarium and sapphsidian was wrapped around his left wrist like an old-fashioned watch. He tapped on the holoscreen, and the device started purring. A few seconds later, a gust of cool air wafted over me.

Jorge sighed with relief, and some of the redness faded from his cheeks. "As you can see, the device comes in quite handy on hot summer days. Even better, it uses a person's own motion and kinetic energy to power itself, thus eliminating the need for a solar battery."

He waved the watch in front of my face. "I'm planning to increase the size and range so that the devices can be wrapped around individual trees and bushes in Promenade Park. That way, we can heat or cool each individual plant, instead of an entire area, which would save the city an enormous amount of energy . . ."

Jorge kept spouting off all the potential uses for and advantages of his new temperature-shielding technology, along with the tweaks he wanted to make to the design, but I tuned out his enthusiastic words. I had never had any sort of mechanical or engineering aptitude, and the only thing I could figure out on a consistent basis was how to kill someone before they killed me. I was wholly unlike my father in that regard, and I supposed my sister too. Vesper probably would have been hanging on Jorge's every word, idea, and statistic, just like my father was.

I grabbed a frosted glass off the tray of a passing servant and downed the contents. A tart lemonade with bright notes of blood orange exploded on my tongue, but the refreshing drink didn't wash the bitterness out of my mouth.

". . . but it's just a prototype right now." Jorge finished his loving description and pulled his coat sleeve down, hiding his wristwatch from sight. "I need to run some more tests and simulations before I scale up the prototype and present the device to the park's board members."

"Of course," I murmured politely.

My father asked Jorge a technical question. The two of them started debating the merits of various shielding technologies currently on the market, and I was finally able to slip away from them. I deposited my empty glass on a servant's tray, then ambled through the crowd, smiling and waving and eavesdropping on every single conversation I could.

The summer solstice might ostensibly be a time for the Regals to relax and celebrate the social season, but it was also a marvelous opportunity to pick up gossip, something my grandmother had trained me to do since birth, all in service to House Zimmer, of course.

"Lady Jane has danced with Lord Austen twice already . . ."

"I hear they're having an affair . . ."

"Forget about them. I'm much more interested in who Vesper Quill's father is . . ."

That snippet of conversation drifted over to my ears, making me stop cold. A few feet away, Lady Livia Invidus was holding court in the center of a gaggle of ladies. I sidled in their direction, pretending to have great difficulty deciding which scrumptious treats to snag from the towers of vanilla-glazed tea cakes, sugar-crusted berries, cucumber-dill sandwiches, spice-rubbed cheeses, and other delicacies lining the refreshment tables.

"It must be some servant or guard," Lady Livia said, continuing her speculation. "Vesper Quill's father couldn't possibly be anyone important, anyone who truly *matters*."

The other ladies murmured their agreement.

House Invidus was among the least powerful Regal Houses, and it sold spy cameras and other tech similar to that produced by House Zimmer. *Bloody copycats*, Wendell had called the House Invidus engineers on more than one occasion, since their products were usually cheap knockoffs of his sturdier, more sophisticated designs. I was inclined to agree with my father, but even someone who spent most of their time copying you could still be a dangerous enemy.

"Why do you say that?" Beatrice asked.

My grandmother glided forward into the circle of women, and the other ladies scattered like mammoth butterflies blown away by a stiff summer breeze to make room for her.

Livia Invidus was in her eighties, just like my grandmother, with pale skin and a teased mane of hair that had been dyed the same garish pea green as her dress. She gave Beatrice an indulgent smile, as though she was talking to a small child who hadn't yet fully grasped the nuances of Regal society.

"We all know what an ambitious climber Nerezza Blackwell is. Surely, if she'd had a child by a prominent Regal lord, she would have revealed the information years ago and used it to her advantage."

"Mmm." Beatrice made a noncommittal reply and fiddled with one of her rings.

Livia's brown eyes narrowed at the telltale motion, and she studied Beatrice a little more closely. "Didn't Wendell know Nerezza back when she first came to Corios? I seem to remember them dancing together at a ball a time or two."

Her voice was mild, but her insinuation was sharper than the cake knives on the refreshment tables. A couple of the ladies sucked in startled gasps, and they all stared at Beatrice, looking for the smallest reaction, crack, and chink in her Regal armor.

My grandmother ignored them all, crooked a finger at a passing servant, and plucked a large glass of lemonade off his tray. To anyone else, she probably looked calm and confident, but her fingers clenched around the fluted stem, and her light blue nails dug into the delicate crystal like she was one more innuendo away from snapping it into pieces.

Beatrice took a slow, dainty sip of her lemonade, making everyone wait, then fixed a pleasant smile on her face and focused on Livia. "Wendell danced with many people when he was younger." She paused and tapped a finger on her lips, as though deep in thought. "As did your son, Charles. Although, if I recall correctly, he was much fonder of your ladies-in-waiting than he ever was of Nerezza."

More gasps rang out, and everyone swung around to stare at Livia, whose cheeks flamed as red as the glass of strawberry punch she was clutching. Her arm drew back ever so slightly, as though she wanted to chuck the glass at my grandmother's head.

Beatrice stared right back at her, and after a few seconds, Livia slowly wilted under my grandmother's cool, steady gaze. Fights between ladies, and lords too, weren't uncommon at Regal events, but Beatrice was far too wealthy and powerful for anyone to take on in such a direct, uncouth manner as tossing punch in her face.

"But you're right about one thing," Beatrice continued in a silky-smooth voice. "Vesper Quill's father is probably some servant or guard Nerezza dallied with once upon a time. No one important. Just like Vesper herself is no one important."

She sniffed. "It was so very gauche of Callus Holloway to

elevate Vesper Quill to *our* status in the first place. I don't know *what* he was thinking, making a lowly lab rat a Regal lady."

Several ladies murmured their agreement, but anger and disgust shot through my stomach, curdling the sweet lemonade I'd drunk earlier.

A lab rat was a common nickname for a worker who toiled away in a corporate facility, building blasters and spaceships for their Regal owners. But Vesper was so much more than that, something I'd discovered the hard way. A couple of months ago, I'd mockingly referred to Vesper as Kyrion's conquest when he and I had been sparring at Castle Caldaren as part of our Arrow training, and she had retaliated by rigging together a couple of blasters and burning my clothes. Then, a few days later, Vesper had killed Julieta Delano, an Arrow traitor who had been secretly working with Rowena Kent.

But Vesper had saved my life—and the lives of countless other Arrows and Imperium soldiers—by exposing Rowena Kent's scheme to sabotage and crash Imperium ships for the Techwave. She had bloody *earned* her Regal title, but to my grandmother, Vesper Quill was a living, breathing scandal that would only bring mockery, scorn, and derision down on House Zimmer.

Now that she had put Livia in her place, Beatrice turned to another lady and asked about her grandchildren. More anger and disgust shot through me. Once again, my grandmother was acting as if it was Regal business as usual, and this momentous revelation hadn't happened and changed the very foundation of our family.

Vesper being my sister was a startling development, to be sure, but ignoring this tough truth wasn't going to be an option for much longer. Sooner or later, someone besides Livia Invidus was going to remember seeing my father with Nerezza in his younger years, start digging, and piece together the scandal. I'd already been scouring the Regal and gossipcast archives for footage of the two of them at a ball, a garden party, or some other event, just like Lady Livia had insinuated. I hadn't found any damning evidence so far, but it was only a matter of time before it surfaced.

The sand was rapidly trickling through the hourglass of this secret, and I had no idea what to do about any of it, especially my father's seething anger and my grandmother's stubborn silence. Like it or not, Vesper was part of our family, and I wanted to bloody *talk* to someone about it. Talking, even if it was only to myself, helped me process things and decide on which actions to take next. And in this case, I had a whole lot to process.

My eavesdropping ruse forgotten, I stalked away from the refreshment tables and went over to the edge of the lawn. A guard standing in front of one of the towering honeysuckle bushes snapped to attention and nodded respectfully. I returned the gesture and prowled past him.

The House Rojillo guards were all dressed in pink poly-plastic armor, and they all had silver blasters and shock batons hooked to their belts, but their postures were lazy and relaxed, much like the Imperium soldiers stationed outside Castle Caldaren. The biggest threat these guards would face tonight would be Regals high on chembonds who didn't want to take no for an answer from the pretty young servants.

I circled the lawn, scanning the guards lined up in front of the bushes and making sure there were no gaps in their formation. The gossipcasters and everyone else might think I was an arrogant idiot, but I took my duties as an Arrow very seriously, and a few days ago, I had reviewed House Rojillo's security protocols for the solstice celebration.

I had sent Lord Jorge several suggestions, including dou-bling the number of guards, moving the security perimeter to the opposite side of the lake, and cutting down some of the bushes on the lawn to provide better sight lines and escape routes in case something went wrong. But Lady Halecia had been downright aghast at the mere thought of thinning out her prize honeysuckles, so Jorge hadn't implemented any of my proposed changes.

Sometimes I thought Regal vanity was going to be the death of us all.

The Rojillos had every right to decide how to protect their own castle, but I knew—*I bloody knew*—they would have made the security changes if Kyrion had suggested them instead of me. The other Regals simply respected—and feared—Kyrion Caldaren far more than they ever had me, thanks in large part to my Zane Zimmer persona. I had no one to blame for that but myself, but frustration still churned in my gut like acid.

Especially since the summer solstice celebration was a prime spot for a Techwave attack.

Dozens of powerful Regals in attendance. A remote location. Scaled-down security that was a far cry from the squads of Imperium soldiers that surrounded Crownpoint and patrolled the Boulevard and Promenade Park. The solstice celebration was the perfect soft target, something I'd mentioned to Callus Holloway, although he too had ignored me, just as the Rojillos had.

They all thought I was paranoid, but they had never been in a Techwave battle like the one on Magma 7. A few months ago, Holloway had sent me, Kyrion, and Julieta Delano to drive the Techwavers out of a metal refinery, but nothing had gone according to plan. Scores of Imperium soldiers and conscripts had been killed, and Julieta had secretly triggered a lava eruption that had almost ended us all. I'd always known the Techwavers were dangerous, but that was the first time I'd realized just how far they were willing to go—and just how many of their own troops they were willing to sacrifice—to topple the Imperium.

So far, the Techwave hadn't dared to launch an attack

anywhere on Corios, but that was something else that was only a matter of time. According to Holloway's spies, the Techwavers were working on a new weapon capable of cutting through a variety of defensive energy shields, from the large ones around ships and buildings to the smaller ones that powerful psions like myself could mentally create to absorb and protect ourselves from blaster fire and the like.

A few weeks ago, Harkin Ocnus, one of the Techwave's top scientists, had kidnapped Vesper from the Quill Corp campus on Temperate 42 and tried to force her to fix the terrorist group's new weapon. Vesper had quickly escaped from Harkin's clutches, but according to Holloway's spies, the Techwave still needed her expertise. They too were hunting her, which was yet another reason I needed to find her before anyone else did. I had no desire to be killed by a weapon engineered by my own sister.

A glimmer of gray caught my eye, and a woman moved out of the shadows surrounding the castle. She stopped underneath a string of bulbs, and the pink glow gilded her long wavy black hair in a soft sheen. A pale gray gown clung to her strong, curvy body like a gauzy cloud, and tiny bits of colored ore glinted on her long skirt. Larger pieces of ore covered her chest, packed tightly together as though she was wearing a jagged, jeweled breastplate.

A thin silver chain gleamed around her neck, with a single bit of ore resting in the hollow of her throat like a tiny shimmering opal. Sparkling silver powder had been dusted over her pale skin, and she looked like a moon goddess who had stepped out of the night sky and down into the garden. Light and dark, and hard and soft, like an artist's study in contrasts.

Wariness coursed through me, as though a pebble had been dropped into the still pool of my mind and was sending ripples of suspicion through my entire body.

Lady Asterin Armas, the woman I was supposed to marry.

THREE

ZANE

Asterin stood stiffly, her hands fisted in her skirt, as if she would rather be anywhere else but here. A sentiment I could well appreciate.

A fifty-something man stepped up beside Asterin. Rigel, her handler, for lack of a better word. His light brown hair was brushed back from his forehead, revealing dark brown eyes and skin that was more ruddy than tan, as if he'd spent just a few minutes too long in the scorching summer sun. His short, muscled body was poured into a dark brown tailcoat that made him look like a mushroom desperately straining to catch a ray of Asterin's radiance.

For the last several weeks, Rigel had been negotiating with my grandmother about which events Asterin and I would attend, if we would sit at the same table, how many times we would dance together, and the like. All our interactions were planned and preapproved, right down to our favorite refreshments. Fun fact: Asterin hated coconut and rhubarb, as did I.

It was all common practice among Imperium Regals looking

to officially tie their offspring together, but these negotiations had been much slower and far more delicate and detailed than most, since Asterin was a member of Erzton society. Marriages and other alliances were not all that common between the two groups, and if Beatrice and Rigel managed to force Asterin and me together, we would be a blueprint, of sorts, for other Regals and Erztonians to follow. Something else that soured my stomach. Regal marriages were often little more than business transactions between Houses, but a small part of me had always hoped that I would at least *care* about whatever woman I eventually married.

You are totally mad for her, aren't you? My own mocking voice drifted through my mind, along with Kyrion's earnest reply: Mad *doesn't even begin to describe it.*

Kyrion had said that about Vesper when he and I had been taking the elevator to the Crownpoint throne room before the midnight ball. At first, I'd scoffed at his confession. How could Kyrion Caldaren ever truly care about anyone other than himself? He was an Imperium Arrow, a moon-cold killer, a bloody proper villain, the same as me. But the certainty in his voice had made me reconsider everything I thought I'd known about my old enemy.

Then, later, in the throne room, I'd seen Kyrion's desperation when he'd been trying to reach Vesper. Even after Dargan Byrne had severely wounded him, Kyrion had done everything in his power to protect Vesper as the two of them had fought their way through the palace. Most people probably would have chalked up his concern to their truebond, since the common theory was that if one person in a bond died, the other person would also soon perish. But Kyrion's raw emotions had hammered against my telepathy again and again, like a throbbing toothache I couldn't ignore, and I'd realized the truth of the matter.

Somehow, some way, Kyrion Caldaren had stumbled into

a truebond with someone he genuinely cared about. The fact that he was connected to my sister was the bitter icing on a tea cake of sour irony.

Perhaps it was our perpetual rivalry, but a tiny part of me couldn't help but want what Kyrion had—someone who was willing to *do* anything, *risk* anything, for him. Although given how much Asterin openly despised me, and my mutual dislike of her, the chances of the two of us forming such a connection were as remote as the blue moons rising in the evening sky.

Beatrice spotted Rigel. She waved at him and started skirting through the crowd toward the handler, who headed in her direction. Asterin watched the two of them for a moment, then spun around and hurried in the opposite direction.

A reluctant smile tugged at the corners of my lips. My sentiments exactly.

Asterin glided through the crowd, nodding and smiling at everyone she passed, but she didn't engage anyone in conversation. Instead, her eyes narrowed as she studied the groups of Regals, as if she was taking the same mental notes about who was talking to whom that I had cataloged earlier. She also paused to study the guards stationed around the lawn, just as I had done.

Asterin Armas might be an Erzton lady, but I had the sneaking suspicion she was also a spy.

But whom she was spying for? The Erzton? Someone else? Or did she devote her intelligence efforts to further her family's House, position, and fortune, as I did mine?

Either way, I didn't—couldn't—trust her, which further fueled my dislike and disdain. I already had enough enemies to deal with. I didn't need to willingly invite another one into my House and my family, much less into my bed. I'd voiced such concerns to my grandmother numerous times, but so far, Beatrice had refused to listen to reason.

Asterin turned away from the guards and moved over to

a refreshment table near the edge of the lawn. She glanced around for a few seconds, then picked up a fluted glass filled with dark purple liquid. Elderberry punch. Despicable stuff. The syrupy-sweet drink always reminded me of the homemade cough syrup that Wendell had forced me to drink whenever I had the slightest hint of a mild cold as a child.

Asterin sniffed the drink and crinkled her nose, but she didn't set the glass down. My eyes narrowed. Elderberry punch wasn't on the list of her favorite refreshments, but she had deliberately picked that glass out of a row of far more palatable punches. I would have bet every single credit in my trust fund that her grabbing that particular drink was a signal to someone. What was Asterin plotting?

Two women sidled out of the crowd and headed over to Asterin. The first woman was wearing a tight gold-sequined gown that brought out her ebony skin, along with her dark brown hair and eyes. Tivona Winslow, the new head of Quill Corp, Vesper's company.

The second woman was much shorter, with light brown skin, hazel eyes, and a sleek bob of black hair that glistened like polished onyx in the evening twilight. She was wearing a feminine version of the traditional Regal tailcoat in a pale, rosy pink, and a stormsword with a gold hilt dangled from the thin gold belt cinched around her waist. Leandra Ferrum, a strong psion and one of the best warriors from House Ferrum, which produced high-quality staffs, crossbows, and other old-fashioned weapons that were often enhanced with lunarium and other minerals.

Tivona and Leandra were clutching glasses of the same foul elderberry punch as Asterin, although all three women set their untouched drinks down on the refreshment table and started speaking in low voices.

Ding! Holloway messaged me again. *Have you started questioning people yet? I want answers, not excuses.*

Well, Holloway wasn't the only one who wanted answers, and for once, I was going to do exactly as he commanded. I stowed my tablet away, plastered another smile on my face, and strutted over to the three women. Party crashing was one of my favorite pastimes as a Regal, right up there with ferreting out information.

"Ladies!" I called out, swaggering my way in between Tivona and Leandra. "So lovely to see you all here tonight."

Tivona let out a derisive snort and crossed her arms over her chest.

"Zane," Leandra drawled, her sardonic tone making her crisp Corios accent more pronounced than usual. "You're looking as ostentatious as ever."

I held my arms out wide and spun around, making my tailcoat flap against my legs. "Is there any other way for such a glorious creature as myself to look?"

"Not if you're a blasted peacock," Asterin muttered.

"I've always been extremely fond of peacocks. We have a whole flock of them in the gardens at Castle Zimmer. They're so delightfully proud and colorful." I smirked at her. "They can also be quite vicious if you don't know how to properly handle them."

Asterin arched an eyebrow. "Oh, I think I could handle you with ease, Lord Zane."

"Perhaps we'll find out, Lady Asterin."

My voice came out a little lower and huskier than I intended, and an unexpected spark of heat flared deep in my chest. Asterin blinked, and for a moment, a bit of awareness, of interest, seemed to flicker in her silvery eyes, but the emotion vanished as quickly as it appeared. In an instant, she had morphed back into a cold, remote moon goddess.

I turned to Tivona. "I'm glad I ran into you, Ms. Winslow. I wanted to speak to you about your former boss, Vesper Quill."

All three women stiffened as though I'd just dropped a

solar grenade at their feet. Tivona's arms plummeted to her sides, Leandra's fingers curled around the golden hilt of her stormsword, and Asterin slipped her hand into a pocket hidden in her voluminous skirt.

I cranked up the wattage on my smile, as if I didn't notice their sudden tension—or weapons. "As the new head of the Arrows, I've been tasked by Callus Holloway to track down Vesper, along with Kyrion Caldaren. I was hoping you could help me with that."

Tivona huffed out an aggravated breath. "As I have told the Imperium investigators *numerous* times, I had no idea that Vesper had a truebond with Kyrion, much less that she planned to escape from Imperium custody. As the new head of Quill Corp, I have cut off Vesper's access to company technology, products, and funds, as ordered by the Imperium." She lifted her chin. "I have followed all of Callus Holloway's orders to the letter of the law. I don't know what more I can do."

"Letter of the law? Yeah, that's about right, considering you've given the bare minimum of information to the Imperium investigators," I replied. "But then again, you are a highly skilled negotiator, Ms. Winslow. You're good at bending the law to suit your own purposes."

Tivona frowned. "Is that an insult or a compliment?"

"Both," I continued in a cheerful voice. "Now, do us all a favor and tell me where Vesper and Kyrion are. I'm very good at being an Arrow, and I'll find them sooner or later. Why not speed up that long, tedious process? Think of the time, energy, and resources you'll save me and the other Arrows. Why, Callus Holloway might even anoint you a Regal lady for your loyal service to the Imperium."

Tivona's features remained smooth, but fury flared in her gaze, and the same emotion rolled off her and scorched my face, as though she was shooting red-hot lasers out of her eyes. My telekinesis was much stronger than my telempathy, so I didn't usually sense other people's emotions so vividly. Not like Kyrion did. Perhaps that was why he was such a broody bastard, having to experience everyone else's feelings all the bloody time.

"As I said before, I have done everything as required by Imperium law," Tivona replied in a calm voice, despite the hot fury still rolling off her. "If you have a problem with that, file a formal complaint against me."

"But you don't agree with Imperium law. You don't think Vesper and Kyrion should be brought back to Corios."

Tivona huffed again. "So Holloway can try to siphon off their magic again? Of course not. It's a barbaric law, one that he engineered to benefit himself, and we all know it."

She was right. The law that any truebonded couple in the Imperium was to be delivered to Holloway was barbaric, cruel, and evil, and I could understand why Kyrion had risked everything to save Vesper and break free of Holloway's crushing grip. He hadn't wanted to be a psionic battery for the greedy siphon the way his parents had been for years. Kyrion might have avoided that gruesome trap for now, but it could still be his fate—and Vesper's too—if someone captured them before I did.

"It might be barbaric, but it *is* the law, and as the head of the Arrows, I am duty-bound to follow the law." I smiled again. "To the letter."

Tivona's lips curled back into a disgusted sneer at my quip, and she shook her head. "I still can't believe that *you* are—"

She cut off her words, but my telepathy let me hear the rest of her loud, strong thought—*that* you *are Vesper's brother*.

A dagger twisted in my gut. Somehow the words never got any easier to hear.

It didn't surprise me that Tivona knew my secret, and I was sure that Leandra and Asterin knew it as well, since the three of them had helped Vesper and Kyrion escape from Crownpoint.

Asterin had attended the midnight ball as herself, while Tivona and Leandra had dressed up like Imperium soldiers and snuck into the palace, as had Daichi Hirano and his uncle, Touma Hirano, a disgraced spelltech who built, sold, and traded all sorts of illegal products on Corios's booming black market. Daichi and Touma were still on Corios, hiding out in the industrial part of the city in an abandoned warehouse they thought no one knew about. I'd found them three days after the midnight ball, and I'd been keeping track of them ever since on the off chance they might lead me to Vesper and Kyrion.

Tivona kept glaring at me, that disgusted look still on her face, as though I was a cockroach who wasn't worthy of being Vesper's brother. She was probably right about that.

Once again, everyone knew my family's secret, but no one was brave or brash or reckless enough to actually *talk* to me about it. My tongue itched with the urge to ask Tivona what Vesper thought of our connection, but I plastered yet another smile on my face and slipped back into my patented Zane Zimmer persona, donning it like a suit of armor to shield myself from any more verbal slings and arrows that might come my way. Too bad it couldn't block out my own troubled thoughts.

"Can't believe I'm what? So handsome? So charming? So utterly irresistible?" I winked at her.

Tivona narrowed her eyes, even more fury sparking in her dark gaze, the emotion hot enough to make a few beads of sweat pop out on the back of my neck.

"Humdrum, perhaps," Leandra drawled. "Condescending, certainly. Arrogant, absolutely."

I gasped and clutched a hand to my heart. "*Humdrum?* You *wound* me, fair lady. To the *core*."

"Your rotten core." Leandra gave me a thin, sharp smile. "Besides, if I ever truly wounded you, then you would know it, Zane."

I grinned and gestured at her stormsword. "Anytime you

want to spar, my training ring at House Zimmer is always open. Why, it would be an honor to host such an accomplished warrior from House Ferrum."

Leandra studied me with suspicion, but my compliment was quite genuine. Leandra Ferrum was one of the best fighters I had ever seen, and her stormsword and psionic abilities made her just as dangerous as I was.

"Don't invite me to your training ring unless you want to be thoroughly beaten," she warned.

I winked at her as well. "It's a date, fair lady."

Leandra rolled her eyes in response.

I turned to Asterin, who was still studying me with cool detachment. I winked at her too, but her expression didn't change, and a strange urge rose in me to think of just the right thing to say to crack through her ice-queen persona.

"Asterin! There you are!" Rigel joined our group.

"Hello, Rigel!" I clapped him on the shoulder as though I was absolutely delighted to see him and not silently cursing his presence.

Despite my hearty gesture, Rigel didn't move a single inch, as if I hadn't even touched him. He smiled at me, his face a benign mask, but his dark brown eyes were cold and assessing, and his arm flexed as though he wanted to snatch my hand off his shoulder and break my fingers one by one.

Rigel might ostensibly be a social handler, but I was willing to bet that he was also a Hammer, one of the Erzton's elite fighters. Asterin's mother and stepfather, Verona and Aldrich Collier, were among the leaders of the Erzton, and they wouldn't send their daughter into Imperium territory without some sort of protection. Although I got the sense that Asterin was more than capable of taking care of herself.

Her hand was still firmly entrenched in her pocket, and I was willing to bet she had some small weapon squirreled away in there. Perhaps she would whip out a blaster and end our unwanted engagement before it even began. Being shot dead by one's potential fiancée would certainly be humiliating, but on the bright side, it would put an end to all my problems, especially what to do about Vesper and Kyrion.

Rigel raised his eyebrows at Asterin in a sharp, pointed expression. Asterin's lips puckered, as though she had just bitten into something sour, but she tipped her head to Tivona and Leandra.

"Lovely to see you both again," she replied in a smooth voice. "I look forward to continuing our conversation later in the evening."

Tivona and Leandra murmured their good-byes, then walked away. Tivona glanced back over her shoulder, her worried gaze darting back and forth between Asterin and me.

I reached out with my power, trying to hear the thoughts of all three women. Like many other psions, I was capable of telepathy, although I used that ability far less than my telekinesis, which was my strongest skill. If I couldn't charm someone with my words or kill them with my stormsword, then I saw no need to listen to their cumbersome thoughts. For the most part, I simply ignored such whispers, although loud, vivid thoughts and feelings could still tweak my psionic senses, like Tivona's earlier disgusted musing about my being Vesper's brother.

But right now, I needed information about Vesper and Kyrion, so I deliberately stretched out with my telepathy, studying each woman in turn. All I sensed from Asterin and Leandra was soft silence, but that was no surprise. Most of the time, I didn't bother trying to eavesdrop on other psions, since they either shielded their minds or their power naturally canceled out my own. But the thoughts of regular humans like Tivona were much easier to sense, so I focused on her.

We're fine, her thought whispered through my mind. *Zane can't possibly know about our arrangements.*

What arrangements had Tivona made with Asterin? Perhaps

their little tête-à-tête hadn't been about Vesper after all. Or at least, not entirely about Vesper. Perhaps as the new head of Quill Corp, Tivona was secretly negotiating some business deal with Asterin and the Erzton.

I made a mental note to dig even deeper into Quill Corp's finances, along with those of Asterin and her family. Beatrice might claim that the Colliers admired the House Zimmer name, fortune, and connections, but the Erztonians' dogged determination to snare me like a rabbit in a trap made me highly suspicious. Noble games aside, there had to be *some* deep, dark reason the Colliers wanted to form an alliance with House Zimmer, especially given Asterin's intense dislike of me.

Beatrice was lurking a few feet behind Rigel. She stared at me, then tilted her head toward the dance floor. I bit back a groan. Suspicions or not, right now, there was no escaping my grandmother's machinations.

I looked at Rigel. "I was just about to ask Lady Asterin to dance. If that meets with your approval?"

Rigel grunted his assent, so I turned to Asterin and held out my hand. She bit her lower lip, once again clearly wanting to be anywhere other than here, but she reluctantly placed her hand in mine.

Despite the humid summer night, her fingers were cool, and I curled my hand around hers, trying to bring some warmth to her soft skin. Asterin tensed, but she didn't pull away.

I led her onto the pink tile floor that had been set up on the grass, and a few other Regals who were already dancing moved aside to make room for us. Fergus was dancing with an older woman from House Gonzalo, and he gave me a knowing grin as Asterin and I stepped toward each other. I glowered at my friend in return, but Fergus just chuckled and spun his partner around.

Several musicians were perched on a nearby hoverdais, and

their loud, lively reel slowed into a soft, sedate waltz. The bulbs strung through the tops of the honeysuckle bushes dimmed, their warm pink glows fading to a cool white, signaling the official start of the solstice ball.

Asterin stared fixedly at a spot over my shoulder, but I looked straight at her. Delicate eyebrows, high cheekbones, heart-shaped lips. She was much lovelier than I remembered from our last tense encounter after the midnight ball when we'd hurled insults and accusations at each other. Or perhaps that was just the romantic atmosphere rubbing off on me, along with the earlier echoes of my father talking about how much he had loved my mother. I had always been a sucker for a grand love story.

Perhaps that was one of the reasons Asterin annoyed me so much—because we would never have the kind of deep mutual care, concern, love, and respect that my parents had shared. Perhaps it was greedy or selfish or even old-fashioned, but I didn't want to settle for anything less than complete trust and true happiness, not even to secure my House's future.

"Why do you keep staring at me?" Asterin snapped, finally looking at me. "Do I have something in my teeth? Is the color of my lipstick not to his lordship's liking? Or am I not cooing and fawning a proper amount over the high and mighty Zane Zimmer?"

I bit back a sigh. We couldn't even get through a simple dance in uncomfortable silence. Still, animosity or not, this was a Regal ball, and I had a role to play, even for a woman who hated me.

"You look beautiful tonight," I said in a cheerful voice. "Then again, you always look beautiful."

Annoyance flickered across Asterin's face. "I suppose you expect me to say how handsome you are in return."

"That is the expected nicety and common reciprocity."

She huffed. "Reciprocity? This whole thing is *reciprocity*."

"Marriages often are, among the Regals."

She huffed again, the sound even more caustic and derisive than before. "Among the Erztonians too, but that doesn't mean I have to like it."

"Then why are you here? Why not tell your parents that you don't want to enter into a marriage contract? Or find another Regal lord whom you can at least tolerate? Surely you have other options."

"It's complicated. And unfortunately, I have only bad options." She muttered the last few words.

A soft chime of confirmation rang through my mind. I wasn't a seer like Vesper, but sometimes my psionic instincts whispered that certain things were true or particular events would come to pass, no matter how outlandish or unlikely they might seem. And right now, my power was agreeing that Asterin had only bad options, which made me even more suspicious and wary. What kind of trouble was she in?

I arched an eyebrow. "I'm a bad option? What a wonderful compliment. I can honestly say no one has ever called me that before."

She rolled her eyes. "Could you try to be serious for one moment?"

"Ah, but there's nothing more serious than a dance with you, Lady Asterin. The mere endeavor is *fraught* with peril. Especially given our audience."

I tilted my head to the side, and she tracked the motion over to Rigel, who was standing beside Beatrice. The two of them had raised their punch glasses to their lips to hide their conversation, but no doubt it revolved around Asterin and me and how soon they could shackle us together.

Asterin muttered a rather colorful curse and glowered in their direction, her silver eyes sparking with heat. Ah, so some hidden fire was buried deep inside the ice queen. What other secrets was she keeping? A surprising urge filled me to uncover them all, even if such an endeavor would only bring more trouble into my already troubled life.

As a Regal lord, and especially as an Arrow, I was good at sizing people up, at figuring out what they wanted, how far they would go to reach their objective, and how much misery they would cause me along the way. Most people fell into three categories: tentative allies, obvious enemies, or dangerous threats to eliminate immediately. So far, Asterin had avoided all my attempts to figure out which one she truly was, which further annoyed me.

I spun Asterin around and away, then drew her back toward me. The motion surprised her, and she stumbled forward. Her hands landed on my shoulders, her fingers digging into my back as she steadied herself.

"It's a good thing you aren't wearing mechanical claws like some of the Erzton Hammers are fond of donning in battle," I drawled. "Or I would be sporting some very deep scratches."

"If my nails were that sharp, I wouldn't waste time scratching you," Asterin cooed right back at me. "I'd go for a quick, decisive slice across your neck."

"You would actually cut my throat and murder me on the dance floor?" I grinned. "How delightfully vicious. Although you'd get blood all over your lovely gown."

She shrugged one shoulder. "A little blood would be worth putting an end to you and this sham of an engagement our families are trying to force us into."

Perhaps I was going about this the wrong way. Perhaps Asterin and I could help each other—and then never have to see each other again.

"There is a way for you to be free of me, and for me to also get what I want."

Asterin regarded me with a wary expression. "What are you proposing?"

Proposing? The mere mention of the word made me shudder

with revulsion, but I kept my voice light and cheerful. "I will tell my grandmother that I will never marry you, no matter what she threatens."

Her expression sharpened. "And in return?"

I gave her my most charming smile. "And in return, all you have to do is tell me where Vesper and Kyrion are."

Her face remained calm, but her fingers dug into my back again. So she *did* know where they were. Excellent. Now all I had to do was pry the information out of her.

"Let me get this straight. You will fight any potential engagement or alliance with my family if I rat out Vesper and Kyrion?" She shook her head. "You really think I'll give in to your petty blackmail? You really think I'll betray my friends just to get what *I* want? You're even more of a callous, clueless jackass than I thought."

I shrugged off her insults. "It's neither blackmail nor a betrayal. You wish to be free of me, and I want to complete my Arrow mission. It's a win-win."

Her mouth gaped, and she stared at me like I was some vile villain she had never encountered before. Then anger sparked in her gaze, making her eyes glint as brightly as the stars above. Disgust surged off her and punched into my chest like a red-hot hammer.

"You're despicable!" she hissed.

"Despicable but effective."

Asterin's jaw snapped shut. She dug her fingers even deeper into my back, and for a moment, I thought she might shove me away, or slap me, or both. Then her fingers relaxed, and she tilted her head to the side, studying me as though she was trying to suss out my secrets the same way I was trying to uncover hers. "What *are* you going to do about Vesper and Kyrion?"

"You didn't answer my question."

"You didn't answer mine," she retorted.

We glared at each other. All around us, the other Regals kept dancing. Asterin and I followed their movements, our steps and bodies stiff with anger.

After several seconds of mutual glowering silence, I huffed out a breath. "I will do exactly what I told you, Tivona, and Leandra. I will find Vesper and Kyrion and bring them back to Corios."

"You know, after you let Kyrion wound you during the midnight ball so he and Vesper could escape from the throne room, I thought there might be a teeny-tiny sliver of decency buried deep, deep, *deep* down inside you." Asterin shook her head again. "But there's no hope for you, is there, Zane?"

"Decidedly not," I chirped. "Especially since I have no idea what you're talking about. Kyrion wounded me fair and square, and I plan to return the favor and gut him like a guppy the next time I see him."

Asterin snorted, clearly not believing my lies. She was right. I *had* let Kyrion wound me that night to make his and Vesper's escape easier, but I would never admit it to anyone, especially not her.

"You saw what Vesper and Kyrion did at Crownpoint," she said, a thoughtful note creeping into her voice. "How much raw power they have. They practically ripped the throne room to pieces with their truebond. Do you really think *you* can capture them? A lone psion with questionable intelligence?"

I shrugged again. "As I said before, I'm very good at being an Arrow."

"A cold-blooded killer," she countered, her lips curling back into a sneer. "One of Callus Holloway's pet assassins."

"Most definitely a killer and absolutely an assassin. Just like Kyrion."

Asterin sneered at me again. "You are *nothing* like Kyrion. He has one important thing you don't. Honor."

I scoffed. "Honor is severely overrated. All it does is let your enemies take advantage of you. Honor gets you killed, nothing more, nothing less."

She grimaced, but for once, she didn't disagree with me. Instead, her face darkened, and her shoulders drooped, as though someone's honor had caused her a great deal of pain. Who had hurt her so badly?

An uncomfortable needle of sympathy pricked my heart, but I ignored the small, niggling sting. Sympathy was something else that would only get you taken advantage of and then promptly killed. Like my sympathy for Vesper and Kyrion, which was the source of many of my current problems—

Ding! My tablet chimed with another message from Holloway, but this time, I ignored the device.

I spun Asterin around and away, following the pattern of the dance, before drawing her back to me again. "But you're right about one thing. I'm nothing like Kyrion." I grinned. "For starters, I'm much more handsome and infinitely more charming."

She snorted again. "Well, you're certainly more arrogant." She tilted her head to the side, her lips puckering in thought. "Are you really that shallow, Zane? Doesn't it bother you at all? What Callus Holloway does to truebonded pairs? What if you were Kyrion? What would you do?"

Anything to protect my partner. The thought whispered through my mind, and the truth of it startled me. Once again, Asterin was right. Truebond or not, if I ever cared about someone as much as Kyrion did about Vesper, then I would do everything in my power to protect that person.

Another memory flickered through my mind. Kyrion staring at Vesper in the throne room, his gaze fierce and adoring and filled with the threat of extreme pain and brutal death for anyone stupid enough to try to separate him from her. But the most surprising thing was Vesper looking back at him the exact same way, as if she cared just as much about the former Arrow as he did about her . . .

"My mother and stepfather have a truebond," Asterin said. Her low, tight voice shattered the memory, and I blinked, coming back to the here and now. I already knew that from Beatrice's research, as well as my own inquiries, but this was the first time Asterin had directly mentioned her family's bond to me.

"Is that why you're so concerned about Vesper and Kyrion? Because you're worried that Holloway will someday try to siphon off your family's power?"

"Yes," she confessed. "And because Vesper and Kyrion are my friends, and I don't want any harm to come to them."

"Oh, yes. I read the reports about how Vesper and Kyrion helped you stop a Techwave attack at the Regenwald Resort you own on Tropics 33." I clucked my tongue. "Foolish of them. If they hadn't stopped to assist you, then the other Arrows and I might have never caught up with them. Vesper and Kyrion could have disappeared to some distant planet, never to be seen or heard from again, instead of now being the two most wanted and notorious fugitives in the Archipelago Galaxy."

"Vesper and Kyrion saved hundreds, probably thousands, of lives by helping me defeat the Techwavers at the resort." More anger and disgust filled Asterin's face. "They did the *right* thing, something you would know absolutely nothing about."

"*Right* is a relative concept that depends entirely on how much someone screws you over. Funny how doing the *right* thing so often involves getting exactly what *you* want, usually at the expense of someone *else*."

Asterin rolled her eyes again, but after a few seconds, her disdain melted away, and a calculating expression filled her face. "What are you *really* going to do about Vesper?"

"I *really* think I've answered this question already."

"Don't play dumb with me. You know *exactly* what I mean, Zane. You have a . . . connection to Vesper."

"Yes, I do, and yet no one seems to be able to actually say the bloody *words* to me," I replied, a snarl creeping into my voice. "Especially not my grandmother and my father. They haven't even admitted it to me yet."

The confession slipped through my lips, and I ground my teeth to shut myself up. The last thing I needed to do was start spilling secrets, especially to someone as untrustworthy as Asterin.

She blinked in surprise. "They're keeping Vesper a secret from you?"

I gave her a curt nod, not trusting myself to speak without revealing even more of my anger and disgust.

Her face softened the tiniest bit. "I know what it's like to be kept in the dark about something so important," she replied in a low voice. "When other people make decisions based on what *they* think is right or best or good for you, instead of letting *you* decide for yourself."

We stared at each other, and something flared between us, some small sparks of understanding and commiseration that melted through the icy artifices we were showing to everyone else—and especially to each other.

"Oh, yes," I agreed, even more anger creeping into my voice. "It is quite annoying to be kept in the dark, and it is getting on my last bloody *nerve*."

Asterin's eyes narrowed in suspicion. "Why? Are you worried Vesper will threaten your position? Usurp your role as the heir to House Zimmer? Take your title and riches away from you?"

Her snide assumptions about my supposed petty jealousy further fueled my anger. "No," I snarled. "I'm not worried about Vesper taking anything away from me."

"Then what are you so upset about?"

"Not what—*who*."

"Okay, if it's not Vesper, then who are you so upset with, Zane?"

"My grandmother," I snarled again. "Because *she* already took something away—she took *Vesper* away from *me*."

Once again, the confession slipped through my lips, even as the hard truth of my words slammed straight into my heart. I *was* angry at my grandmother—angrier than I had ever been at her before.

Beatrice had schemed and plotted and moved me around like a pawn my entire life, and I had let her because it was all part of the Regal game. My grandmother had always insisted her actions were for the greater good of our family, but keeping the secret of Vesper from my father and me hadn't been for the greater good. Oh, Beatrice might claim it had been to protect House Zimmer, but really, all it had done was serve her own selfish need to squash the potential scandal and hang on to her exalted status among the Regals.

Asterin's eyebrows shot up in surprise, as though I'd said something wholly unexpected. With anyone else, I could be Zane Zimmer, self-absorbed Regal lord and arrogant idiot Arrow. But not with her, not about this.

Asterin eyed me as though I was a rabid sand lion, and she wasn't sure if I was going to rear up and bite her or not. She slowly leaned forward and lowered her voice. "Vesper is *your* sister, Zane. *You* decide how you feel about her, not your grandmother. Just like *you* decide what to do about her, not Callus Holloway."

"Don't you think I *know* that?" I snapped.

"Then start acting like it," she snapped right back at me.

We stopped dancing, both of us glaring at each other.

Another couple jostled into Asterin from behind, propelling her forward into my arms. Her body bumped up against mine, her softer curves melting into my harder planes. The subtle scent of her soap flooded my nose, smelling tart and sweet, like summer blackberries. My anger vanished, and something hot, hungry, and wholly unexpected erupted in my chest, like a dragon breathing fire deep inside me.

Asterin froze, her gaze locking with mine. Her lips parted, and I suddenly wondered what they tasted like, what *she* tasted like—

The same clumsy couple jostled us again, this time knocking Asterin out of my arms. She stumbled, and I gripped her elbow until she steadied herself. We faced each other again. All around us, the other couples slowed their dance steps as the music wound down.

"My offer still stands," I said. "Tell me where Vesper and Kyrion are, and I'll put an end to our families' scheming. You have my word."

"Your word is as empty as all your other pretty promises." She jerked her elbow out of my light grip. "I don't care what our families are plotting. You're arrogant and infuriating and swagger around like an overconfident peacock. I will *never* get engaged to you, just like I will never tell you anything about Vesper and Kyrion."

"And you're cold and remote and distant as a Frozon moon," I growled right back at her. "Someone is going to find Vesper and Kyrion sooner or later. So do us both a favor and tell me where they are."

Her eyes narrowed, and she tilted her head to the side again, as though she was seeing much more than I wanted her to, much more than I ever wanted anyone to see. "Our mutual disdain aside, you should figure out what *you* want to do, Zane, instead of doing what everyone else expects and demands of you. Maybe you'll have better blasted luck with it than I have."

A grim, lopsided smile split her lips, but the expression quickly iced over into another cold glower.

"Either way, Vesper is a good person, and she deserves far better than the likes of you."

Asterin gave me a stiff, shallow curtsy, the bare minimum that protocol dictated and not an inch lower. Then she whirled around and vanished into the crowd, leaving me standing alone on the dance floor.

FOUR

ZANE

sterin might have stormed away, but her words kept echoing in my mind. *Vesper is* your *sister, Zane. You decide how you feel about her.*

But that was the problem—I didn't know *how* I felt about Vesper. Everything was a jumble in my mind. My grandmother's stubborn silence. My father's angry shock. My own simmering disgust. Vesper's unknown feelings. Each person and emotion yanked me in a different direction, but in the end, they all just circled around each other, like a viper eating its own tail again and again.

But like it or not, Vesper *was* my sister, and I was going to have to do something about that inescapable fact. I was going to have to choose a side and commit to a course of action—good, bad, or ugly.

The music ramped up again. Several Regals whirled by, and more than a few titters sounded, since I was still standing in the middle of the dance floor like a lovestruck fool. Fergus eyed me with concern, still swaying with his partner. I plastered my usual smile on my face, then gave a deep, low bow to my friend and all the other watchers, accompanied by a showy hand flourish.

The titters grew a little louder as I left the dance floor, but the mockery didn't bother me. Even though I had spent my whole life around these people, none of them truly knew me. Asterin had learned more about me in the few minutes we'd been dancing than the Regal lords and ladies had in all the time I'd spent with them over the years. Just like Vesper had learned more about me during our blitzer ride back to Corios than any of the Arrows had in all the time I'd served with them—

Beatrice planted herself in my path, causing me to pull up short. "Where are you going?"

I jerked my head at the refreshment tables. "To get a drink. Something a lot stronger than lemonade."

She let out an exasperated sigh and shook her head, making the blue opals nestled in her silver hair sway back and forth. "You need to find Asterin. Rigel told me that he hasn't seen any gift from you this evening."

I tapped my finger over my heart where the lunarium jewelry box was still hidden in my coat pocket. "What did you want me to do? Whip this out in the middle of the dance floor, get down on one knee, and declare my intentions?"

A thoughtful look filled my grandmother's face. "Well, it wouldn't have been *terrible*, as far as proposals go. I've seen far worse at Regal balls. Singing. Poetry. Puppet shows." She shuddered at that last one.

It took me a moment to unclench my jaw. "As I've told you many times, Asterin despises me, and I have the same mutual disdain for her."

"Bah!" Beatrice flicked her fingers. "Disdain is of little importance in the grand scheme of things. Do you know what *is* important?"

Before I could answer, she finished her own thought. "All

the mineral rights on all the Frozon moons that Asterin controls. Minerals that your father needs for his inventions, that House Zimmer workers and production plants need to keep pace with the other Regals."

A dull headache spurted to life inside my skull. Beatrice had been drilling my duty as the heir to House Zimmer into my head for as long as I could remember, but right now, everything inside me was rebelling at her words.

"So you're going to trade my life, freedom, happiness, and future children for minerals. Charming," I drawled. "And here I thought that family *always* came first. Although in this case, you are clearly putting the House Zimmer coffers first. A bit hypocritical, don't you think?"

My grandmother flicked her fingers again, dismissing my accusations. "Sometimes sacrifices must be made, even by family, for the greater good of the House."

"*Sacrifices?* Is that what you're calling them these days?"

Her eyebrows drew together in puzzlement, but after a few seconds, her gaze slowly sharpened. She knew we weren't talking about my giving the necklace to Asterin. Not anymore.

Beatrice opened her mouth, but I sliced my hand through the air, cutting her off. "Fine. I'll find Asterin and deliver your precious solstice gift. After all, I'm just another one of your pawns, and it's time for me to get into position and play my part yet again. Right?"

Before she could answer, I spun around on my heel and stalked away.

A few folks called out to me, but one look at my clenched jaw and angry scowl had them seeking more pleasant company. Even Fergus and the other House Zimmer servants steered clear of me.

My gaze snapped back and forth, but I didn't spot Asterin anywhere on the lawn. Perhaps she had gone into the castle in search of some peace and quiet. I could certainly use some of that right now, so I slipped through the first archway I came to and moved through a shadowy courtyard, heading toward one of the castle's entrances.

Ding! I growled with annoyance, but I stopped, pulled out my tablet, and read the latest message from Holloway. *Have you discovered where they are hiding?*

This time, I sent a reply. *Nothing yet. I'll keep questioning people.*

I want progress, not more of your empty excuses.

I growled again and shoved the tablet back into my pocket. Everyone wanted something tonight, and nothing I did made anyone happy. Fantastic. Well, I was going to find Asterin, shove the necklace box at her, and be done with it. Then I was getting a bloody drink, Holloway's messages and threats be damned.

I stomped toward the door, but I had only taken a few steps when two guards rounded the side of the castle. One of them took up a position beside the door, but the other man hung back, then angled his body away and discreetly pulled a tablet out of his pocket, as though he didn't want the first man to see what he was doing.

His furtive movements struck me as extremely odd, and I slowed down, softened my angry, noisy steps, and took a closer look at him. Dark red hair, dark eyes, ruddy skin, a long, sharp nose, and a pointed chin. I frowned. I didn't remember seeing his face among the House Rojillo guard rosters that I'd reviewed a few days ago.

As an Arrow, I'd been in a lot of bad situations over the years, and I'd learned to listen to my instincts, psionic and otherwise. Right now, all those instincts were whispering that something was wrong, so instead of barreling forward, I stopped beside a large white wooden trellis covered with honeysuckle vines and slid back into the shadows.

"Come on, Silas," the first guard called out. "We need to get back in position."

"Sure thing, Thompson," the other man chirped in a voice that was dripping with fake sincerity.

My eyes narrowed. I recognized that breezy, disarming tone. I'd used it myself, usually right before I shoved my stormsword into someone's back. Oh, yeah. This guy was *definitely* up to something.

Silas slid his tablet into his pocket, then plucked an object off his belt and held it down at his side. At first, I couldn't see what it was, but then he moved forward, and a shock baton glinted a dull silver in his fingers.

Before I could shout a warning, Silas surged forward and shoved his shock baton into the first guard's neck. Thompson never had a chance. He grunted and convulsed a few times before collapsing in a heap on the ground.

Silas slid his shock baton back onto his belt, then grabbed the unconscious guard's ankles and quickly dragged him behind a stone planter bristling with honeysuckle vines. He stepped back around the planter, pulled a small comm device out of his pocket, and nestled it into his right ear.

"Exterior guard neutralized," he said in a low voice. "Moving to first objective."

I didn't hear whatever response was made, but Silas nodded, opened the door, and slipped into the castle.

I yanked my own tablet out of my pocket, but a message on the screen indicated that I didn't have a signal anymore. I muttered a curse. Silas—and whoever was working with him—must be jamming all other communications, which meant I had no way to warn Beatrice or Wendell or get any help from the House Rojillo guards.

I could return to the ball, find Lord Jorge, and tell him what was happening, but that would take far too long and draw too much attention. The last thing I needed was for the guests to panic. Besides, Castle Rojillo was a massive, sprawling structure, and if I didn't follow Silas now, then I risked losing him for good. And given my current foul mood and simmering frustration of the past few weeks, I wanted to hit something, and Silas's face would make an excellent punching bag.

I shoved my tablet back into my pocket, slid out of the shadows, and hurried over to Thompson, the unconscious guard. I made sure he was still breathing, but there was nothing else I could do for him right now, so I went through the same door Silas had used.

I stepped into a long, wide corridor made of glossy pink stone. Tall, skinny tables were spaced down the corridor, each one boasting a crystal vase, a quartz statue, or some other expensive, useless knickknack. Hoverglobes bobbed gently up and down in midair, although the pink flames inside had been turned down low, and they created far more shadows than they banished.

Silas was about fifty feet ahead of me, quickly and quietly moving from one doorway to the next and peering into all the rooms he passed. I followed along behind him, careful to keep my footsteps as soft as his. It wasn't hard to do, since husky murmurs and passionate cries echoed out of many of the darkened rooms.

Some of the Regals had already indulged in chembonds, which were just what their name implied: chemicals that mentally connected people for a brief period of time. Several different types of chembonds existed, but they were most commonly used for sex, especially at society balls. Clothes rasped, furniture squeaked, and low, throaty moans bounced off the walls as the Regals enthusiastically pleasured themselves and their partners.

Silas stopped and peered into another room. Three loud,

enthusiastic voices drifted out of that area, indicating that every-one involved was having a grand time. Silas pulled out his tablet and angled the device in their direction. Perhaps his in-tentions were more greedy than nefarious. Gossipcasters—and blackmailers—often snuck into places they weren't supposed to be to get juicy scoops on illicit Regal dalliances.

But instead of snapping a photo or recording a video, Silas lowered his tablet, ignored the passionate sounds, and veered to the left through an archway. I frowned. If he wasn't here for gossip or blackmail, then what was he doing? Where was he going?

I hurried forward and peered through the archway. Silas crossed an interior courtyard, then used a key card to open a locked door and stepped through to the other side. I pulled my stormsword off my belt and followed him.

The door had locked behind the rogue guard, so I tapped on one of my opal cuff links three times, then held it up to the card reader. The opal burned a bright blue, and a tiny electromag-netic pulse zinged out of the stone, frying the keypad. One of my father's more useful inventions.

The door clicked open. I winced at the unwanted noise, but I cautiously stepped into another corridor. Instead of smooth pink stone, this area was made of sterile gray tile. Sturdy metal doors were set into the thick walls, and there was nary a knick-knack in sight. This was the industrial heart of the castle, where Jorge Rojillo created his designs, and it was an eerie mirror to a similar area where my father worked in Castle Zimmer.

Silas wasn't here for gossip or blackmail. He had his eye on a much larger prize—he was a thief here to steal House Rojillo technology.

Corporate espionage among the Regal Houses was quite common. Every Regal family was always searching for new ways to raise themselves up and undercut their rivals, and stealing proprietary designs while Lord Jorge was hosting the summer solstice celebration was a clever way to accomplish both goals. But which House was Silas working for? And what tech was he after? House Rojillo made all sorts of things, from air purifiers to shielding grids for homes and ships to the climate-control wristwatch Jorge had shown me earlier.

Silas had vanished, so I crept down the corridor and glanced through the small permaglass windows set into the doors. Supply closets, tool depositories, cleaning stations. There was no sign of Silas in any of the rooms, and all the doors were locked, so I kept moving forward, my stormsword still clutched in my hand. The lunarium blade shimmered with a pale blue light, painting the gray tile corridor in a ghostly glow.

I glanced up, but no cameras were embedded in the ceilings, which meant no one was watching me or Silas creep around the corridors. Another security suggestion I'd made that Lord Jorge had failed to implement, but the lack of cameras wasn't unusual. Most Regals relied on guards, alarms, locked doors, and energy shields to keep them safe, and few wanted cameras recording their comings and goings inside their own homes.

I stopped at a junction, my gaze flicking between three different corridors. They all looked the same, but Jorge had sent me the castle schematics to review for the solstice celebration, so I knew that his main research-and-development lab was off to the left. That would be my first stop if I was here to steal valuable tech for a rival House, so I headed in that direction.

A few twists and turns later, I reached another junction, a wide corridor that wrapped around a large interior space. Still no sign or sound of Silas. I glanced left, then right, and my gaze snagged on a nearby keypad. The light there glowed a steady green, and the door beside it was cracked open.

I lowered my stormsword to my side. I didn't want the sword's glow to give away my location, so I loosened my grip on the hilt, and the lunarium blade dimmed in response. I cocked my head to the side, listening, but I didn't hear anything, so I tiptoed over to the door, grabbed the handle, and gently pulled it open. The door glided back without making a sound, and I silently slipped into the space beyond.

It was a large R&D lab. Tile counters studded with sinks hugged one wall, while clear, polyplastic workstations clustered together in the center of the wide, open space. Terminals covered the workstations, along with laser cutters, hammers, and pliers. Stray bolts, screws, and wires were also strewn across the surfaces, glinting like dull, jagged stars. Reusable plastipapers were stacked in folders, and gelpens clustered together in coffee mugs, but overall, the area was neat and tidy. The cool air smelled of a citrusy cleaner, along with a faint, underlying note of melted metal. I wiggled my nose from side to side to hold back a sneeze.

Microscopes, vises, and other tools perched on wheeled chrome carts nestled in between welding stations and larger pieces of machinery that were scattered around the perimeter of the lab. Gray tarps covered much of the machinery, making the equipment look like bulky ghosts that were about to break free of the walls and haunt the area.

But the centerpiece of the lab was the floor-to-ceiling lockers covered with heavy-duty metal grates that lined the back wall. Plastic and glass glimmered behind the grates, although given the dim lighting and distance, I couldn't make out what projects and prototypes were stored back there. All the lockers were shut tight, and the lights on their keypads burned a bright, steady red.

My gaze flicked from one side of the lab to the other and back again. I still didn't see anyone, but a faint presence tweaked my psionic senses.

Someone was in here.

I put my back to the wall and silently tiptoed forward, moving deeper into the R&D lab. When I reached the closest counter, I crouched down beside it so that whoever was in here couldn't see me anymore, then headed toward the back corner of the lab. I stopped beside a metal cart and waited several seconds, but the intruder didn't move, and the only sound was the whisper of recycled air circulating through the lab. If Silas wouldn't come and play, I would just have to find him. I grinned. I had always loved hide-and-seek.

I tightened my grip on my stormsword and fed a tiny bit of my psion power into the weapon. The lunarium blade shimmered a pale blue in response. I lowered the sword, then angled the blade toward the right, casting the faint blue glow across the floor like an impromptu flashlight.

Hiding your body in the shadows was easy. Hiding your feet on the floor was much more difficult.

I slowly and carefully shone the lunarium blade across the tiles, but all I saw were the curved wheels and square legs of the carts and workstations, along with a few wayward pieces of plastipaper and several alarmingly large dust bunnies that looked like mutant monsters growing in the shadows.

The right side of the lab was empty. I stopped to listen, but once again, I only heard the faint hiss of the air-conditioning system. Next, I reached out with my psion power. Once again that presence tweaked my mind, like a cool finger tickling the back of my brain, but I didn't sense any loud thoughts or strong emotions from the other person. No sweaty panic, no heart-pounding worry, no stomach-churning dread.

My respect for Silas rose another notch. By this point, most people would have done *something* to break the tense silence, even if it was just shifting on their feet, but he seemed to have ice in his veins, the same as me.

I moved my stormsword to the left, still using the lunarium blade as a makeshift flashlight to peer across the floor. The pale blue glow illuminated four legs on a workstation about thirty feet away from me, along with five legs on a nearby stool . . .

Wait. I stopped and shone the light back at the stool. The

intruder yanked his foot back, stepping deeper into the shadows, but it was too late.

Triumph flashed through me. *Got you!*

I didn't make a sound, but Silas must have known that he'd been spotted because a shadowy figure detached itself from a piece of machinery and bolted toward the lab door. I cursed, shot to my feet, and headed in that direction.

The intruder had a straight, open, easy path toward the exit, but several workstations were standing in my way. Instead of wasting valuable time weaving around the stations, I grabbed hold of the side of the closest one, vaulted myself up onto it, and then used my telekinesis to slide across the slick polyplastic surface and drop down to the opposite side.

I repeated that process over and over, knocking terminals, tools, plastipapers, folders, cups, and gelpens off the stations in my slip-sliding wake and making the objects *ping-ping-ping* across the tile floor. I grimaced at the noise and kept going.

The figure darted out the open lab door. I slid over one last workstation, landed on my feet, and chased after him.

The shadow was already halfway down the corridor, but I sprinted in that direction, using my telekinesis to make my steps longer than normal, until I was bounding, rather than running. The intruder was quick and light on his feet, but I was rapidly cutting down the distance between us.

The thief ran by a hoverglobe, which illuminated the dark gray cloak covering his body. No wonder he had melted into the shadows in the workshop . . .

I frowned. Wait. Silas had been wearing House Rojillo armor when I'd last seen him. Where had he gotten that cloak from?

But it didn't really matter. The cloak might have helped him hide before, but all that long, flowing fabric was going to doom him now.

I put on an extra burst of speed, bounded forward, and grabbed the back of the cloak. The shadowy figure let out a startled cry, but I fisted my hand in the sleek fabric and jerked him to the side, using my telekinesis to slam him into the closest wall.

Silas bounced off the gray tile, yanked something out of his pocket, and whirled around. A small blaster glinted a wicked silver in the semidarkness. I snapped up my sword and lunged forward, ready to drive the blade through his heart and pin him to the wall like a mammoth butterfly.

The intruder jerked to the side, making the hood of the cloak fall down and revealing his—no, her—features.

Black hair, silver eyes, furious expression.

The shadow wasn't Silas, the rogue guard.

It was Asterin Armas.

FIVE

ZANE

I stopped my strike, my stormsword hovering three inches away from Asterin's heart. She also stopped, although her blaster remained leveled at my chest.

"What in all the stars are you doing here?" I snapped. "This is a restricted area. None of the solstice guests are allowed near Jorge's labs."

She lifted her chin and gave me a cool look. "I could ask you the same thing, Zane."

We continued our staring contest, our weapons still up and at the ready. Several seconds ticked by in tense, hostile silence.

Finally, I blew out a breath, stepped back, and lowered my sword. Asterin was as stubborn as I was, so threats wouldn't work on her. Besides, I had no desire to get shot in the chest and see exactly how powerful her compact blaster was.

Asterin eyed me a moment longer, but she slowly lowered the blaster to her side, then slipped the weapon into a pocket in her long gray skirt.

"I *knew* you had a weapon tucked away in there."

Asterin smoothed down her skirt. "It seemed prudent when dancing with you."

I arched an eyebrow. "I wondered if you might shoot me in the middle of the dance floor. That would be one way to thwart our families' matchmaking efforts."

Asterin snorted. "We will never be *matched.*"

I thought of the dazzling opal necklace still nestled in the jewelry box in my coat pocket. "You are severely underestimating my grandmother's determination."

Anger flashed in her eyes. "No one else's determination decides *my* fate."

A grudging bit of respect filled me. Asterin Armas had plenty of fighting spirit, although going up against Beatrice Zimmer almost always ended up being a losing battle.

"Matchmaking aside, that still doesn't explain why you're sneaking around this part of the castle." My eyes narrowed. "Has your husband-hunting these past several months just been a cover? A clever way for you to infiltrate Regal castles to steal their technology?"

Asterin stiffened, and a bit of guilt flickered across her face before she could hide it. My chest twisted with something that felt a lot like disappointment. Despite my suspicions about her ulterior motives, I'd wanted to be wrong about her. I wasn't quite sure why.

I kept firing questions at her. "Is the rogue guard working for you? What are the two of you after?"

A confused frown creased Asterin's face. "What rogue guard?"

"I believe Lord Zane is referring to me," a deep, snide voice called out.

Asterin and I both spun to the side.

Silas was now standing in the corridor, still wearing House Rojillo armor, along with black gloves. A shock baton dangled from his belt, but somewhere along the way, he'd acquired a much more impressive weapon: a large silver hand cannon that was pointed straight at me.

Silas reached over and hit a button on his left glove. An instant later, his armor started rippling, as though it was made of water instead of tough, strong, solid polyplastic. The ripples darkened, and within seconds, his armor had shifted from House Rojillo pink to a shiny black, belt, boots, and all. Neat trick.

Still keeping his cannon aimed at me, Silas let out a low whistle, as though he was the master of the castle summoning a pack of dogs to his side. A series of loud, familiar *clanks* rang out, and four figures appeared in the corridor behind him. The hulking figures were encased in sleek black polymetal armor, and compound green eyes glowed in their heads, making them resemble oversize insects.

Beside me, Asterin tensed. "Black Scarabs," she whispered.

Her shock punched into my stomach, then churned alongside my own worry. This wasn't some corporate-espionage scheme to steal proprietary designs from House Rojillo. It was so much worse than that.

The Techwave was here.

I flipped through my mental catalog of Techwave members, trying to connect Silas's face with his real name, whatever it was, but I didn't come up with a match. Not surprising. The Techwave was all about compartmentalization, and not much was known about the group's senior members and leadership. Even Callus Holloway, with all his spies, hadn't been able to penetrate the terrorist organization's upper echelon, much less figure out what its ultimate plot was against the Imperium.

Silas grinned at me. "Have I rendered the great Zane Zimmer speechless? How delightful."

A hint of the familiar Corios accent tinged his voice, signaling that he had spent some time among the Regals. Perhaps he was a former guard who had defected from the Imperium and gone over to the Techwave. Either way, working for the Techies was going to be the last mistake he ever made.

I tightened my grip on my stormsword. "What are you doing here?"

"Getting what I came for." Silas jerked the cannon at me. "You can come along quietly, and I might let you live. Or you can cause trouble and die where you stand. Your choice, Arrow."

His cold brown gaze flicked over to Asterin, and his grin took on a sharp, predatory edge. "After all, I only need one hostage."

I growled and stepped forward, putting myself between Asterin and the Techwavers. I might not like Asterin, and she clearly had nefarious reasons for being here, but she was still a guest, the same as everyone else at the solstice celebration. I was an Arrow, sworn to protect the Imperium, and I would be damned if I let this bastard and his mechanized troops hurt her.

Silas rolled his eyes, as if my defiance was expected but still annoying. "Kill him."

Two of the Black Scarabs rushed forward, their metal feet clanking against the floor in a rolling, ominous rhythm.

I snapped up my sword. "Run!" I yelled at Asterin. "Get help!"

She shook her head, yanked her blaster out of her pocket, and stepped up beside me. "You need help right now!"

Bloody stubborn spy. She was right, although I would never admit it. Still, I was determined to protect her, so I sprinted ahead, taking the fight away from Asterin and to the Black Scarabs.

At the last instant, right before I would have plowed straight into the troops, I dropped into a slide across the slick tile floor like an athlete trying to reach the goal line. I put some telekinesis into the motion and ducked my head, zipping right through the wide-spread legs of the closest Black Scarab.

The second I was past the mechanized troop, I dug the toe of my right boot into the floor, stopping my slide and popping back up onto my feet. Then, still going low, I spun back around and sliced my stormsword through the Scarab's legs, right above its knee joints. The lunarium blade easily sheared through the tough black polymetal, spitting hot blue sparks everywhere.

The top of the Scarab lumbered forward, as if the machine thought its legs were still attached to the rest of its body, and the two halves started sliding away from each other. I snapped up my hand and used my telekinesis to fling the top half of the broken Scarab into the one standing next to it and then dashed them both into the wall.

Pew! Pew! Pew!

Bright gray blaster bolts zinged down the corridor and slammed into the two Scarabs. Bits and pieces of metal cracked off their armor, and the fluids inside the machines splattered onto the floor, the wall, and even the ceiling, like drops of glistening, onyx-black blood.

Asterin stepped forward, still firing her blaster. *Pew! Pew! Pew!*

More bolts slammed into the two Scarabs. The green glows in their eyes finally dimmed and died, and both troops slumped to the floor like broken toys.

Despite the situation, I grinned at Asterin. *Nice shooting.*

She must have heard my telepathic thought, because she grinned back at me, her white teeth flashing in a beautiful, vicious expression. Then her eyes widened. "Behind you!"

I whipped to the side. Another Black Scarab lunged forward and rammed its fist into my temple. White stars exploded in my field of vision like a supernova, the intense pain blotting out everything else.

"I don't have a shot!" Asterin shouted, but her voice sounded tinny and far away. "Zane! Zane, move—"

Her voice abruptly cut off, although more clanks sounded, along with the dim sounds of a struggle. Asterin must be fighting the other Scarab.

I snarled and lifted my sword, trying to blink the stars away so I could help her, but I was too slow, and the Scarab beside me rammed its fist into my temple again.

More pain spiked through my head and rushed out through the rest of my body in a tingling numbness. My legs buckled, my ass hit the floor, and my stormsword tumbled out of my hand. In an instant, I was flat on my back, trying to blink through the stars still exploding in my eyes.

Footsteps sounded. A shadow loomed over me, and Silas's face swam into view. "Good-bye, Arrow."

The Techwave leader gave me a dispassionate look, then raised his hand cannon and pulled the trigger.

Green energy erupted out of the weapon and slammed straight into my heart. The blast washed over me, zipping through my veins like an unstoppable current of hot, electric agony, even as that supernova of stars exploded in my eyes again, bigger and brighter than before.

I screamed once, or at least I thought I did, before everything abruptly snapped to black.

SIX

ZANE

"Zane? Zane!"

A voice kept yelling my name over and over, but not in an admiring *Zane-you're-such-an-amazing-warrior* way. Or in a passionate *Zane-you're-such-a-fantastic-lover* way. Not even in an indulgent *Zane-your-shampoo-com-mercial-is-so-silly* way. No, worry punctuated this voice, and the sound of my own name beat against my ears like a frantic hammer.

I tried to open my eyes, but they wouldn't cooperate, and pain kept zipping through my chest like someone was dragging hot daggers across my skin over and over. All I wanted to do was let go and fall back into the peaceful black void of un-consciousness, but that frantic voice wouldn't stop shouting my name. Even more surprising was the sensation that flooded my brain, like a cold little pebble was angrily vibrating in the deep, still pool of my mind and stubbornly keeping me awake, whether I wanted to be or not.

My eyes still didn't want to open, so I reached for my power.

In addition to being a strong telekinetic, I also excelled at creating psionic shields, which let me ignore extreme injuries and keep fighting instead of being crippled by the agonizing pain. My shields were some of the strongest among the Arrows, and I could take far more wounds than most before my power gave out and I finally dropped.

I imagined erecting a permaglass barrier in my mind, a clear, sturdy wall with me on one side and all the hot, pounding pain on the other. Slowly, my psionic shield solidified, and the pain died down to a more manageable level of warm throbbing. I also tried to shove that annoying little vibrating pebble behind my psionic shield, but it refused to budge.

I cracked my eyes open, not quite sure where I was or what was going on. To my surprise, I was lying on my side like a battered test dummy in my father's workshop. Green smoke wafted up off my ruined tailcoat, and an acrid, electrical stench invaded my nose, slithered down my throat, and coated my mouth like I'd just swallowed a handful of ash from a Magma planet.

Ah, yes. Now I remembered. I'd been shot point-blank in the chest with a Techwave hand cannon. Wonderful.

"Zane? Zane!" that voice kept shouting at me.

I opened my eyes a sliver wider. The remaining two Black Scarabs had overpowered Asterin, had grabbed her arms, and were now dragging her down the corridor toward Silas, who was still clutching his hand cannon.

"Let's go!" Silas ordered, backpedaling all the while. "We need to reach our primary objective before someone comes across the dead Arrow. Bring her. Now!"

He whirled around and jogged down the corridor. Asterin kept yelling and struggling, but the two Black Scarabs easily pulled her along and rounded a corner, and they all vanished from view.

I tried to jump to my feet, but the pain spewed up like red-hot lava against the permaglass wall in my mind, threatening to melt right through my psionic shield, so I slumped back down and rested my cheek on the cool tile floor.

Baby steps, Zane. Baby steps.

Sweat streamed down my face, but I gritted my teeth and forced myself to slowly sit upright. Gray stars blinked in warning in my eyes, but I kept breathing, and the stars slowly faded away.

Fuck. That had *hurt*.

I glanced down. Silas's cannon had scorched an impressive hole in my tailcoat and shirt and severely blistered my skin underneath. But why hadn't the energy blasted right through my body? I patted my chest, and my fingers brushed up against something that was nestled over my heart: the jewelry box I'd been carrying around all evening.

I pulled the box out of my charred coat. The lunarium shimmered with heat, and tiny flecks of blue, red, green, and other colors blazed in the stone, making it resemble a fire opal. The box had absorbed and deflected just enough of the cannon's energy to keep it from killing me, the same way the lunarium blade of my stormsword would soak up and swat away blaster bolts in a battle.

I would have laughed at the bloody irony if it wouldn't have hurt so much.

The jewelry box might have saved my life, but sharp needles of pain stabbed through my chest with every breath, indicating that I had at least a couple of cracked ribs to go along with my burned, blistered skin.

I tucked the box back into my ruined coat, then fumbled for my belt. My shaking fingers slipped off the slick black leather a few times, but I finally managed to pluck a small silver injector out of a slot. I rammed the injector into my right thigh, and a skinbond flooded my body, the healing chemicals zipping through my veins in a cool, soothing wave.

I drew in a breath, and air filled my lungs a little more easily than before. The skinbond also eased the hot, pulsing ache in my skull, although that strange little vibration kept tweaking my mind, like someone was plucking a bowstring in the bottom of my brain again and again. No doubt I had a concussion to go along with my scorched skin and cracked ribs. Wonderful.

Zane? Zane!

Asterin's voice ripped through my mind. I blinked in surprise. Was she trying to reach me telepathically? Could she even do that? According to Beatrice's research, Asterin had some sort of power, although my grandmother hadn't been able to pin down exactly what kind of psion Asterin was or what abilities she might have. Yet another mystery surrounding the Erzton lady.

I listened, but Asterin's voice didn't sound again, either in my mind or out loud. The industrial part of the castle had soundproof walls, and the only noise was the steady hiss of the air-conditioning system. Perhaps the concussion had made me hallucinate her voice.

Either way, I needed to find her, so I plucked a second skinbond injector off my belt and rammed it into my thigh. Another wave of healing chemicals flooded my body, easing more of my injuries. My mind cleared, and I was able to wall off the rest of the pain and pack it all down into a little permaglass box, where it would stay until I released it—or died, whichever came first.

I braced one hand on the wall, then slowly staggered up and onto my feet. Asterin's blaster was lying on the floor, so I scooped it up and hooked it to my belt. The Techwavers had also left behind my stormsword. I reached out with my telekinesis and waggled my fingers, and the sword flew up off the tile and zipped over into my hand.

As soon as my fingers closed around the silver hilt, renewed energy flowed through my body, and the blade glowed a pale blue, as though the innate power stored deep inside the lunarium was refueling and refreshing my own psionic abilities.

I twirled my sword around in my hand, straightened up, and hurried down the corridor. I had to reach Asterin before Silas decided he didn't need a hostage after all.

I hadn't been incapacitated for more than a few minutes, but that was long enough to give the Techwavers a big head start. I moved from one corridor to the next, trying to figure out where Silas had taken Asterin, but the soundproofed walls cloaked their passage, even the loud, clanking footsteps of the Black Scarabs.

No one else seemed to realize that the castle had been breached, because no alarms blared, and I didn't pass a single guard, which meant they were all outside on the lawn with the Regals.

I was on my own.

In some ways, I had always been on my own. Sure, I had my father and my grandmother and my numerous cousins, along with the other members of House Zimmer, but the weight of being a Regal, especially an heir, had always fallen on me since I was an only child—

I shook my head. Nope, not an only child. Not anymore. Now I had a sister.

Perhaps I was more concussed than I'd thought because I couldn't stop thinking about Vesper. What would my little sister have done if she were here? Probably broken into one of the R&D labs, grabbed a bunch of disparate parts and pieces, and engineered them into the perfect weapon to defeat Silas and his Black Scarabs.

A grim smile tugged at my lips. Right now, I would have happily used one of Vesper's unorthodox creations if it meant killing the Techwavers and saving Asterin.

I reached a junction where the corridor split left and right. Both were empty and quiet, and I couldn't tell which direction Silas had gone. But I only had two choices, so I headed toward the left. That corridor led deeper into the industrial side of the castle where more of Jorge's labs were located and thus the most likely place for the Techwaver to steal something.

I took three steps in that direction before I abruptly stopped.

No.

The word popped into my mind, firm and insistent. What was that? Had Asterin . . . just whispered a thought to me? But it didn't feel like a telepathic thought from someone else, more like a nudge from my own power. Besides, Asterin most likely thought I was dead, just like Silas did, so she would have no reason to try to telepathically send a message to me.

I shook my head again and took another step toward the left.

No.

The word bloomed in my mind again, and a sense of frustrating wrongness swept over me, as though I was trying to shove my foot into a boot that was two sizes too small. I didn't know what was happening, what my psionic abilities were trying to tell me, but I spun around in the opposite direction and stepped toward the other corridor.

Yes.

The wrongness vanished, replaced by a buoyant rightness, so I tightened my grip on my sword and hurried in that direction.

I followed the twists and turns of the corridor and went up some stairs, stopping every so often to look and listen, but I still didn't hear anything that would tell me exactly where the Techwavers had gone—

Clank-clank.

Clank-clank.

The sounds echoed down the corridor. Definitely Black

Scarab footsteps, coming from somewhere up ahead and over to my . . . right.

I moved from one corridor to the next, my strides becoming quicker and longer with each passing second. I reached another junction and slowed down. Despite my growing concern for Asterin, I forced myself to stop and peer around the corner.

Up ahead, the gray tile gave way to pink stone, indicating that I had moved from the industrial part of the castle back into the old-fashioned quarters where the Rojillo family resided. I frowned. Why would Silas bypass all the R&D labs with their proprietary projects, designs, and technology and come to this section of the castle? What was he after?

I eased down the corridor. I didn't hear any more footsteps, but the Black Scarabs had definitely come this way. In the middle of the corridor, a door was creaking back and forth, barely clinging to its hinges. Deep grooves were visible in the door, as though a Black Scarab had punched its spiked fingers deep into the thick wood and forcibly ripped the barrier open.

I crept up to the broken door. No sounds drifted out of the room, so I lifted my sword a little higher, drew in a breath, and rushed forward straight into . . . a library.

My gaze darted left and right, but the area was empty. No Silas, no Black Scarabs, and no Asterin.

Frowning, I lowered my sword and took a closer look. Wooden cases bristling with books, statues, vases, and other knickknacks. Several comfortable, overstuffed chairs arranged in front of a small cold fireplace. Framed family portraits lining the stone mantel above. Gold, silver, and bronze-colored honeysuckles sitting in pots on a high, wide shelf, their tendrils draping all the way down to the floor like a glittering, metallic waterfall.

My frown deepened. If Silas was here to steal House Rojillo tech, then why hadn't he gone into the main R&D lab that Asterin had breached earlier? The most valuable prototypes were stored there, along with terminals and servers that would contain scores of potential designs and other sensitive information. This library looked like all the other ones I'd seen in the castle. Why, it wasn't even the largest one I'd passed, and I didn't spot anything worth stealing—

A glimmer of gray caught my eye. Asterin's cloak was lying in a crumpled heap in front of one of the bookcases. I hurried over and snatched up the cloak, but no blood stained the fine fabric. Silas and the Black Scarabs hadn't hurt her—yet.

But the longer I looked at the cloak, the more it bothered me. Earlier, outside the R&D lab, I'd yanked hard on the garment, but it had remained securely wrapped around Asterin's body. Now here it was, just lying in the library. Why? One of the Black Scarabs could have ripped it off . . . or perhaps Asterin had deliberately taken it off and left it behind as some sort of clue.

I dropped the cloak and looked at the bookcase. A small antique sundial was squatting on one of the shelves, although it was turned at a strange angle, with part of the silver casing hanging over the edge of the wood. Curious, I took hold of the sundial. It wouldn't lift off the shelf, but it seemed like it would twist to the right . . .

Click.

Part of the bookcase popped forward, then rolled to the side, revealing a small alcove with a standing desk and a lone terminal tucked inside. My eyes narrowed. Smart of Jorge to hide a terminal in this library, although his cleverness had backfired. Silas must have decided it would be far easier to access this terminal instead of trying to breach the R&D lab, although Asterin had managed it—

Beep-beep-beep.

I glanced down. A small black grenade was lying below the terminal, a red light flashing on the side. Terrific. Just what I needed. A booby trap.

I cursed and shoved the sliding bookcase back into position as far as it would go, in hopes that it would partially contain the impending explosion. Then I whirled around. I was too deep in the library to escape before the grenade detonated, so I rushed toward the largest, sturdiest-looking piece of furniture, a wooden desk tucked in the far corner next to the fireplace.

I leaped up and slid across the top of the desk, sending plastipapers and gelpens flying in all directions. A small, potted silver honeysuckle also flew off the desktop, smacked against the fireplace, and broke apart, spewing dirt and pottery everywhere.

I landed on the opposite side and shoved the accompanying chair out of the way, sending it banging back into the wall. Then I ducked down and scrambled beneath the desk, plastering myself up against the side closest to the wall and the farthest away from the grenade, hoping, hoping, hoping that the thick wood would be strong enough to shield me from the coming blast—

BOOM!

SEVEN

ZANE

The explosion ripped through the library.

Bright light. Intense heat. Incredible noise. All of it blasting through everything in its path, including me.

The light, heat, and noise went on and on and on in a continuous, flaming, furious roar, making me feel like I was hunkering down on the surface of a sun. All around me, the sides of the desk warmed, as though I was trapped inside a wooden oven that was going to roast me alive. Sweat dripped down my face, and acrid smoke clogged my lungs, making it hard to breathe. I hunkered down a little more, pressing myself into a tight ball and as flat against the floor as I could manage at the same time.

All the while, the light, heat, and noise just kept going on and on and on . . .

Slowly, the roar faded away, along with the concussive waves of fire and force. I crawled out from beneath the desk and stood up. Intense ringing sounded in my ears, as though dozens of alarms were jangling all around my head.

Disoriented, I wobbled back and forth on my feet, my stormsword glowing a weak, watery blue in my hand. A thick cloud of smoke billowed over me, and my violent coughing reignited the painful ache in my cracked ribs, along with the pounding pain in my head, despite the skinbond injectors I'd used earlier.

I blinked a few times, and the library settled back into focus. What was left of it, anyway.

The explosion had reduced the wooden cases to smoldering splinters, and loose pages from the burned books drifted through the air like charred gray snowflakes. The framed portraits on the fireplace mantel were piles of ash, the gold frames melted to the wall. All the plants had been reduced to blackened husks, and flames flickered here and there, greedily consuming everything they touched.

Debris had slammed into the desk I'd taken cover behind, and long, jagged bits of crystal, metal, and stone stuck out of the sides like makeshift spears. If the wood had been an inch thinner, I would have been skewered to death. I shuddered and spun away from it.

In addition to the ruined furniture, the grenade had shattered all the windows and blown out half of the back wall, revealing the blue moons and bright stars of the summer solstice sky.

Some of the roaring finally faded from my ears, but in the distance, screams and shouts rose up. Everyone at the solstice celebration had heard the explosion, which meant Silas wouldn't care about quietly sneaking around anymore. No, the only thing he would be concerned with now was his escape, and he would order his remaining Black Scarabs to cut down anyone who got in his way.

Knowing the Techwave's penchant for destruction, Silas wouldn't waste this opportunity, and he would wade right through the center of the solstice celebration and try to hurt— and kill—as many people as possible. My gut clenched at the thought of my father and grandmother getting cut down by Black Scarabs. It would be terror, chaos, and carnage—unless I stopped it.

I tightened my grip on my sword, swerved around the many fires burning in the library, and staggered over to the blown-out wall. I had to reach the lawn, and my family, before it was too late.

The explosion had decimated this part of the library, which was on the castle's second level, and created a gigantic pile of rubble that stretched all the way down to the ground some twenty feet below. I hopped from one chunk of stone to another, as though I was surfing down a rippling wave of rocks. The pieces of stone slipped, slid, and shattered under my boots, but I made it down the rubble pile without falling and breaking my neck.

The instant my feet were on solid ground, I sprinted forward, rounding a corner of the castle and heading toward the back lawn where the solstice celebration was taking place. Up ahead, the tall honeysuckle bushes loomed into view, the bulbs still glowing in the thick branches. Hope sparked inside me. Perhaps I was wrong, and Silas had slipped out of the castle another way, without targeting the guests—

Pew! Pew! Pew!

Bright red blaster fire erupted, several of the bulbs shattered, and more shouts and screams sounded. I blocked out my cracked ribs, along with all my other aches and pains, once again shoving them all into that permaglass box buried deep inside my mind. Then I sucked in a breath and forced myself to run faster.

My boots churned up grass, along with the rich earth underneath. I didn't have time to skirt around the honeysuckle bushes, so I plunged straight into the closest one. The rough branches scraped across my hands and face, while the sticky blossoms clutched at my clothes like pink leeches, but I hacked them all away with my stormsword.

I burst through to the other side and had to stop short to keep from tripping over a House Rojillo guard. He was lying face up on the ground, his mouth gaping in surprise, his body still convulsing from the violent electric shock he'd received. The poor man hadn't even had a chance to draw his blaster to defend himself. Neither had any of the other guards scattered on the ground nearby like twitching oversize pink petals.

My gut twisted with fresh dread. Silas and the Black Scarabs had already neutralized the perimeter guards, which meant there was no one left to stop them from attacking the solstice guests.

I couldn't help any of the fallen guards, so I skirted around them and hacked my way through another honeysuckle bush. Then another one . . . then another . . .

Slowly but surely, the lawn came into view, and each new glimpse of the chaos and destruction sent another arrow of worry shooting straight through my heart.

Overturned game booths with props and prizes spilling out of their busted sides. Splintered tables and shattered chairs. Platters of food littering the ground like colorful mush. Broken bulbs spewing sparks. Smashed sun- and moon-shaped crystals glinting like jagged diamond shards in the trampled grass. Fires burning around the drinks table, fueled by the alcoholic punches that had soaked the grass.

I gritted my teeth and worked harder and faster, hacking through another honeysuckle bush . . . and another one . . . and another one . . .

Finally, I broke through the last bush and made it out onto the lawn.

Roughly a dozen Black Scarabs were rampaging through the

ruined remains of the solstice celebration, smashing through whatever was in their path. How in all the stars had that many Scarabs gotten onto the lawn so quickly?

In the distance, water erupted like a geyser, and a Black Scarab trudged up out of the lake and onto the grass. Silas had hidden his Scarabs at the bottom of the lake, just outside the security perimeter, and then waited for the right moment to activate them. Clever.

The remaining House Rojillo guards had taken up defensive positions behind the overturned game booths and were firing their blasters at the Scarabs, although the machines shrugged off most of the bolts and kept advancing. Rigel was also firing a blaster, although his weapon was punching large, devastating holes in the Scarabs, just like Asterin's blaster had earlier. Yells and shouts zipped through the air, along with the continued *pew! pew! pew!* of blaster fire, and the sulfuric stench of electricity hung over the lawn like a hot, smoking blanket.

A Scarab rushed up on the blind side of a guard who was shooting at another machine. I stepped in that direction and opened my mouth to shout a warning.

Too late.

The Scarab latched on to the guard with one of its mechanical hands, hoisted the screaming man high into the air, and then tossed him aside as though he was as light as a piece of plastipaper. The guard slammed into one of the honeysuckle bushes, crashed through the branches and flowers, and dropped to the ground, although I couldn't tell if he was unconscious or dead.

Most of the Regals and servants were running past the guards toward the relative safety of the castle, although a few folks were trapped on the lawn and crouched down behind the splintered tables near the dance floor—including my family.

Beatrice was on her knees, a long, sharp cake knife gleaming in her fingers, while Fergus was standing over her, brandishing the broken, jagged stem of a crystal flute. My father was in front of them, clutching a fork in one hand and a sparking string of bulbs in the other. A few feet away, the head of one of the Black Scarabs swiveled from side to side, as though it was searching for a specific target. Its glowing green eyes locked on my father, and the machine spun in that direction and rapidly advanced toward him, as if it had finally seen its objective.

My heart seized in my chest, but I raced in that direction. I swung my stormsword out in front of me like a machete, hacking through the splintered tables, busted chairs, and everything else in my path. Glasses shattered under my boots, hot sparks sizzled over my body, and blaster bolts zinged by my head, but I shut out all the noise, chaos, and commotion and calculated the distance between myself and the Scarab and the distance between the Scarab and my family.

I wasn't going to make it in time.

I quickened my pace and snapped my left hand out in front of me. I reached for my telekinesis, but my head was still pounding from the blows I'd taken, as well as the force of the library explosion, and I couldn't quite get a grip on my power.

Even worse, the permaglass box in my mind was slowly cracking under the strain of trying to contain all my pain. If my psionic shield shattered, then the full force and fury of my injuries would roar through my mind and body unchecked, and I wouldn't be able to help anyone, not even myself. I gritted my teeth, shored up the shield as best I could, and kept going, pushing my body to its maximum ability.

The Black Scarab stopped in front of my father and stretched its hands out. My gut clenched. If the Scarab latched on to my father, the mechanized troop could easily use its superior strength to literally rip him limb from limb. I'd seen it happen to Imperium soldiers during the battle on Magma 7 a few months ago. Bitter bile rose in my throat, but I swallowed it down and forced myself to run even faster.

"Die, you bastard!" my father screamed.

Wendell ducked the Scarab's awkward grab and darted forward. My father popped back upright, then shoved the sparking string of lights into an open joint on the Scarab's breastplate and skewered one of the bulbs with the fork, pinning everything in place. He spun around and ducked down. Both he and Fergus put their bodies over my grandmother's, shielding her—

Bewp! Bewp! Bewp!

One after another, the bulbs exploded, sounding strangely like a series of loud burps. Pink fire flashed, and the Scarab glanced down at its chest. The improvised explosive had blasted off the outer layer of the Scarab's armor, revealing the mass of wires and other circuitry underneath. But the mechanized troop was only wounded, not dead, and it lifted its head, fixed its glowing green eyes on my father, and stretched out its hands to squeeze the life out of him.

I put on a final burst of speed, stepped in front of my father, and shoved my sword deep into the open mass of wires. Green sparks shot out of the Scarab's innards, while flashes of blue fire spewed out of my lunarium blade, adding to the smoking mass of melting metal and liquefying plastic inside the Scarab's chest.

"Die, you bastard!" I hissed, repeating my father's words.

I twisted my sizzling sword even deeper into the Scarab's chest. Wires, hydraulics, and bolts snapped, cracked, and popped inside the machine, but it was still standing, so I yanked my blade free, then whirled around and lopped the Scarab's head off its shoulders.

More things snapped, cracked, and popped inside the machine, which let out a plaintive wail that sounded eerily human. The Scarab stretched its right hand out to me, as if begging for help, but I stepped back, and the headless machine slowly pitched forward and clattered to the ground at my feet.

I swiped the sweat off my forehead and looked over my shoulder. My father straightened up, and his relief blasted over me like a cool breeze.

"We're okay!" Wendell yelled. "Go! Help the others!"

I nodded and rushed forward. Rigel and the House Rojillo guards had killed a few of the Scarabs, but the vast majority were still rampaging across the lawn. I moved from one Scarab to another, driving my stormsword into their backs, cutting their legs out from under their bodies, chopping their heads off their shoulders, and killing them however I could.

I spun around, growled, and lifted my sword to engage another Scarab . . .

A bright flare erupted in the center of the Scarab's chest, as though a molten, neon-pink flower was blooming in the middle of its black polymetal armor. The pink intensified, burning brighter and hotter, then abruptly vanished. The Scarab toppled forward, revealing Leandra Ferrum and the glowing stormsword in her hand.

Leandra grinned at me, then twirled her sword around, making pink streaks of lightning crackle around the lunarium blade. "Go!" she yelled. "I can kill the rest of these mechanical bastards!"

She rushed over to another Scarab and lunged back and forth at a dizzying pace, slicing off both its arms before whirling all the way around and chopping off its head in one smooth motion. Tivona Winslow clutched a blaster and followed Leandra, protecting the warrior's blind side.

I spun around, surveying the lawn. Rigel and the House Rojillo guards had surrounded the other Scarabs and were slowly but surely shooting them to pieces with their blasters, but there was still another enemy I needed to find and destroy.

Where was Silas? What had he done with Asterin?

Down by the lake, a glimmer of gray caught my eye, like

a shooting star streaking across the water and answering my silent questions. Asterin was struggling with a Black Scarab that was dragging her along the pink sandy shore. Silas was there too, leading the way and doing something with his tablet.

"Asterin!" I yelled.

There was no way she could have heard me above the screams, shouts, and blaster fire still zinging across the lawn, but her head turned, and she stared right at me, her gaze locking with mine.

In that moment, everything slowed down and crystallized, as though I had hit a button, frozen a video mid-scene, and zoomed in on the specific details I wanted to see. Asterin's long black hair whipping around her face. The glitter shimmering on her skin. The fury flashing in her silver eyes, making them glow even more brightly than the stars above.

Then the Black Scarab dragged her into the woods, shattering the scene, and she vanished from view like a moon that had disappeared for the night.

My heart hammered in my chest, the roar in my ears drowning out everything else. I sucked down a breath and started running again.

EIGHT

ZANE

Behind me, more shouts rang out, but they were the human cries of the House Rojillo guards and not the mechanized clanks of the Black Scarabs. Rigel and the guards should be able to help Leandra and Tivona kill the remaining machines and secure the lawn, so I kept running.

I needed to get to Asterin.

Silas had to have some kind of transport waiting nearby to take him to safety. If he managed to drag Asterin onto a ship, there would be no helping her. The Techwave abducting an Erzton lady from a Regal celebration would create a galactic incident that would further strain relations between the Erzton and the Imperium. No doubt Callus Holloway would blame me for the whole fiasco, and he might even make good on his threats to end me once and for all. I needed to save Asterin to save myself, along with my family.

Besides, Asterin might be a thief and a spy, but she didn't deserve to die at the Techwave's hands—or worse, end up in one of their labs as a gruesome experiment.

I picked up my pace, sprinting straight toward the woods and watching for any telltale flares of cannon or blaster fire. If I were Silas, I would have stationed at least a few Black Scarabs in the woods to cover my escape, but no bright pulses of energy erupted, and I made it to the edge of the trees without encountering any resistance.

As much as I longed to charge forward, I forced myself to slow down, soften my steps, and ease into the woods. Coniferous trees with gray trunks and silvery needles crowded together, casting out long, spindly, arrow-shaped shadows, while wild honeysuckle vines snaked along the forest floor like sticky green vipers with pink heads. The scent of the evergreens mixed with that of the flowers, creating a sharp yet sweet perfume.

Up on the lawn, shouts and yells drifted through the air, but the thick screen of trees and branches muffled most of the sounds and encased the woods in an eerie bubble of relative quiet. Overhead, the blue moons and stars were shining brightly and gilding everything in a gloomy gray sheen.

Still clutching my stormsword, I tiptoed from one tree to the next, moving deeper and deeper into the woods. In addition to reviewing the blueprints for Castle Rojillo, I'd also studied maps of the surrounding area. A small clearing was nestled in the center of the woods that was just large enough for a blitzer to safely land. That's where I would go if I were trying to escape as quickly as possible, so I veered in that direction.

I stopped every so often to look and listen, but no glowing green eyes appeared, and no telltale clanks rang out. Silas must have sent most of the Black Scarabs to the lawn to cause as much destruction as possible and help cover his escape.

Since the woods weren't teeming with Scarabs, I quickened my pace. Less than two minutes later, the trees and bushes thinned out, and the clearing came into view. A small blitzer was squatting in the open space, its hull painted the same grays and greens of the surrounding woods to help it better blend in with the landscape.

Silas was standing close to the bottom of the open cargo-bay ramp, hitting buttons on his tablet. The hand cannon he had shot me with earlier was dangling from a thick strap that was slung across his chest. A few feet away, Asterin was trying to peel a Black Scarab's fingers off her neck. The mechanized troop gave her a violent shake. Asterin froze, but her anger and frustration rippled across the clearing and tickled my telempathy.

A sharp, warning beep sounded. Silas stuffed his tablet into his pocket, then spun around, grabbed his cannon, and snapped it up. "You tripped my perimeter alarm," he called out. "Show yourself—or I start shooting."

Still clutching my stormsword, I slowly eased into the clearing, my mind whirring with plans and options, considering all the players in this deadly game.

Silas blinked a couple of times, as if I was a ghost who'd come back to haunt him. "How are you still alive?" he snarled. "I shot you point-blank in the chest!"

"Just lucky, I guess." I jerked my chin at the cannon in his hands. "Or perhaps your little toy doesn't work as well as you think it does."

His lips pinched together in frustration, and agreement flickered in his eyes before he was able to smooth out his expression. So there *was* a problem with the new Techwave weapon, just as Holloway's spies had theorized. That must be why Silas had only electrocuted the House Rojillo guards instead of killing them outright. His cannon hadn't had enough juice to finish the job. Good to know, although the information wouldn't help me right now.

"That's far enough, Arrow," Silas warned. "Unless you want my Scarab to snap her ladyship's pretty neck."

The Black Scarab slid its fingers around to the back of

Asterin's neck, so that she was standing in front of it, a clear human shield. Asterin grimaced at being maneuvered around like a doll, but she didn't make a sound of protest. Instead, her sharp, searching gaze flicked from me to Silas to the surrounding trees, and I could almost see the mental calculations going on in her eyes as she thought up and discarded plans to free herself from the Scarab's tight grip.

I slid forward another step. If I could just get a little closer, I could kill the Black Scarab . . .

"Stop!" Silas snarled. "Now!"

"Okay, okay, I'm stopping," I called out, raising my arms in mock surrender.

Silas waggled his cannon at me. "Drop your sword on the ground. Your blaster too."

I gently tossed my stormsword out in front of me, using a bit of telekinesis to make it land in exactly the position I wanted. Then I carefully plucked the blaster off my belt and held it up where everyone could see it.

"Actually, this isn't my blaster. It's hers." I jerked my chin at Asterin. "What a lovely little weapon to carry around in your pocket, my lady. Nice and compact and deadly."

"I don't care whose weapon it is," Silas snarled. "Toss it down. Slowly."

I stared at Asterin, making sure her attention was fixed on me. Then I winked at her and tossed the blaster out in front of me. Once again, I used a bit of telekinesis to make it land exactly where I wanted.

Be ready, I whispered in my mind.

Silas didn't react, indicating that he hadn't heard my telepathic thought, but Asterin's eyes narrowed. She didn't send a thought back to me, but she blinked twice in rapid succession almost as if she was saying *okay*. She didn't know exactly what I had in mind, but she was ready to move.

I looked past Asterin, reached out with my psion power, and

scanned the blitzer, but no loud thoughts, strong emotions, or other presences tickled my telepathy. No one else was on board the ship. No more Scarabs either. If Silas had had more mechanized troops, they would have been down here on the ground with him, already tearing me to pieces.

"What kind of tech did you steal from Lord Jorge?" I asked. "Surely the Techwave doesn't need the latest, greatest air purifier. Unless the stench of all those polymetal troops is finally going to General Ocnus's head."

Silas chuckled. "Ocnus does love his toy soldiers, but no, Lord Jorge had something far more interesting and useful. Too bad you won't live long enough to figure out what it is."

He took better aim at me with his cannon, and I raised my hands a little higher.

"Forget the stolen tech. Let's make a deal. Release Lady Asterin, and I'll let you and your Scarab board that blitzer and fly away free and clear."

I meant what I said. Whether they were friend or foe, people were always more important than things. I needed to save Asterin first. Then I could separate Silas from his hand cannon, and then his limbs from the rest of his body.

"In case you've forgotten, *I'm* the one with the superior weapon." He shook his head. "You really are as dumb, arrogant, and idiotic as everyone says."

"Aw, do I have a fan club inside the Techwave? How marvelous. I'll have to send you all some bottles of shampoo from my latest commercial. Galactic Suds for Studs. I think you'll love it. Should add some extra shine to your hair."

I gave him my most charming smile. Silas glowered back at me, his finger curling around the cannon's trigger, but I kept right on smiling. I might be arrogant, but he was the real idiot. If there was one thing that I had learned from being an Arrow, it was that villains always—*always*—had to brag about how bloody strong, smart, and deadly they were. Silas should have already fired his weapon, as many times as it took to kill me, instead of dishing out insults and hinting at the Techwave's nefarious plans. And people thought I was a show-off. Please.

"Fuck your shampoo, and fuck the Imperium," Silas growled. "As for Lady Asterin, I'll be taking her with me to make sure your Imperium friends don't shoot me out of the sky. They wouldn't dare kill an Erztonian lady. The Imperium needs the Erzton and all its raw resources too badly to risk damaging relations with the other group."

Not a bad escape plan, as far as these things went, but he was severely underestimating Callus Holloway. Erzton relations be damned. The Imperium leader absolutely loathed General Orion Ocnus, and Holloway would shoot any ship with any passenger out of any sky if he thought it would benefit him and hurt Ocnus and the Techwave in the smallest way. Besides, Holloway could always lay the blame squarely on me and then execute me for my supposed incompetence to try to weasel his way back into the Erztonians' good graces. He'd done such things before to other Arrows who had failed to complete their missions.

Silas was also severely underestimating Asterin. I still didn't know what kind of psion she was or what abilities she might have, but she wouldn't go down without a fight. The two of us were remarkably similar that way.

"How fascinating it is to listen to two men discuss my fate," Asterin drawled in a sardonic voice. "Are you going to explain being a hostage to me next?"

I huffed, as though she had greatly insulted me. "I would never *dare* to do such a thing, my lady."

"Oh, shut up," Silas snapped, his gaze flicking over to Asterin. "Erzton, Imperium, it doesn't matter. You're just a spoiled bitch like all the Regals, and soon, you'll die screaming just like all the Regals will too."

Anticipation rippled through his voice, along with a dark

promise that made my gut clench. What was the Techwave planning? And why did they need Jorge Rojillo's technology to achieve their goal?

Silas jerked his head at the Scarab. "Get her on the ship. Now. I'll take care of our uninvited guest."

The Scarab's head bobbed up and down, and it moved backward, dragging Asterin along with it. Her eyes locked with mine, worry and determination flaring in her bright, steady gaze.

I stepped forward. "Take me instead. I'm a much more valuable hostage."

I was speaking to Silas, but my gaze darted over to the Black Scarab. It was ten feet away from the base of the cargo-bay ramp and still lumbering backward, its oversize, unblinking green eyes fixed on me.

Nine feet . . . seven feet . . . five feet . . .

Three . . . two . . . one . . .

The Scarab stepped back, and its foot banged into the bottom of the cargo-bay ramp. The mechanized troop wobbled at the unexpected obstacle and slight change in elevation, and its hand slipped off the back of Asterin's neck and dropped to her shoulder.

Move! Now! I sent the thought to Asterin.

I snapped my hand forward, used my telekinesis to grab Asterin's blaster from the ground, and sent it spinning in her direction. She couldn't break free of the Scarab's grip on her left shoulder, but she lunged forward and stretched out her right arm.

A wave of psion power arced out to meet my own, almost as if I was physically passing the blaster to her, and the weapon zipped over into Asterin's hand. As soon as her fingers closed around the small, compact blaster, she snapped it up, jerked her body to the side, and shot the Black Scarab three times in the head.

Pew! Pew! Pew!

The Scarab wobbled on its feet for a second, then pitched forward. Asterin leaped out of the way of the falling machine, then whirled around and aimed her blaster at Silas.

The Techwaver snarled and spun toward her, his finger curling back on the trigger to fire his cannon.

I snapped my hand forward again. This time, my stormsword flew up off the ground, zipped through the air, and sliced across Silas's shoulder. He screamed, but he didn't go down, and he didn't drop his weapon. Instead, Silas swung back around to me, aimed his cannon at my chest, and started to pull the trigger—

Pew! Pew! Pew!

Asterin shot him three times with her blaster. Silas screamed again, but he crumpled to the ground, the cannon sliding out of his hands.

Asterin stepped forward, looming over Silas, her blaster aimed at his head.

I hurried over to her. "Are you okay?"

"Fine," she growled. "Now that this bastard is down."

Silas was lying flat on his back. Blood dripped down his arm from where my sword had sliced him, but that was a minor wound compared with the three blaster holes Asterin had punched in his chest. The acrid stench of his fried flesh mixed with the electrical burn of the blaster bolts that still filled the air, along with a faint coppery tang of blood. Even if I'd had another skinbond injector on my belt, it wouldn't have been enough to save him.

"Any last words?" I asked, crouching down beside the dying man. "Care to confess what the Techwave stole? Now that your mission has failed?"

Silas grinned. Blood stained his teeth a dark, ominous crimson and trickled out of the side of his mouth. "I didn't fail. I already . . . sent the data. Now we have . . . almost everything we need . . . to finally destroy . . . the Imperium . . ."

His head lolled to the side, his chest stilled, and his last breath escaped in a raspy sigh.

I muttered a curse and stood up. "Is it true? Did he have time to send data to the rest of the Techwave?"

Asterin shook her head. "I don't know. After he shot you, we went straight to a library. He opened a hidden compartment in a bookcase and connected his tablet to a terminal. I couldn't see what he accessed or who he might have sent it to."

I raked a hand through my hair and started pacing back and forth beside his body.

"What do you think the Techwave is plotting?" Asterin asked, worry creeping into her voice.

I stopped pacing and stared down at Silas. Perhaps it was my imagination, but his lips seemed to be curved in a smug smile, as though he had beaten us, even in death. "Nothing good."

I searched Silas's body, but other than his tablet, he wasn't carrying anything noteworthy. I slid the device into my pocket, then picked up his hand cannon and hooked it to my belt so I could study the Techwave's new weapon later. Finally, I retrieved my stormsword from where it had landed on the ground and boarded the blitzer while Asterin stood guard with her blaster outside.

The blitzer was a common Techwave model, and my quick search didn't turn up any obvious clues, other than the jamming device Silas had used to block signals around Castle Rojillo. I shut off the device, then sent the ship's location to the closest squad of Imperium guards so they could come and secure the scene.

Once that was done, the Imperium investigators, engineers, and scientists would go over the Techwave ship from top to bottom. Perhaps they would find something I'd missed, but I doubted it. Silas had already sent the stolen House Rojillo tech to his superiors, and it was doubtful that he'd left any important information behind on the blitzer.

I stomped down the open cargo-bay ramp, frustration pounding through my body with every loud, harsh, clanging step.

Asterin was still keeping watch outside, her blaster trained on the trees around the ship. "Find anything?"

"Nothing," I growled.

She nodded, let out a tired sigh, and lowered her blaster. Then she reached up with her left hand and gingerly probed the side of her head, hissing a bit. A large reddish bruise had puffed up there, as though she had tucked one of the pink-star honeysuckle blossoms behind her ear.

"You're hurt." An unexpected bit of concern shot through me, along with more than a little guilt. "I'm sorry, but I don't have any more skinbonds."

Asterin shrugged. "It's nothing. Just a little sore. I don't even remember bumping into anything." She pointed at my head and made a small circle with her index finger. "Besides, I'm not the one who got punched in the face by a Black Scarab."

The skinbonds might have dulled the sharpest pains of my many injuries, but the goose egg on my temple was throbbing again. I reinforced my psionic shield, adding another layer to that glass box in my mind. The last thing I needed was for the box to shatter here in the middle of the woods and for me not to be able to walk back to the castle.

Asterin's gaze flicked over my body before landing on the large black hole scorched into my jacket. "Are you sure you're okay?"

I puffed up my chest. "Just fine and dandy. It takes more than a point-blank cannon blast to the chest to keep Zane Zimmer down for long."

She snorted. "Talking about yourself in the third person is *so* pretentious."

"Haven't you heard? I'm Zane Zimmer, the Imperium's most arrogant idiot."

A thoughtful look filled her face. "You're a lot of things, but an idiot is not one of them."

I gasped, clutched my hand to my chest, and staggered back in mock shock. "My dear Lady Asterin, is that, dare I say it, a *compliment?*"

She rolled her eyes, but a small, reluctant smile curved the corners of her lips. "You must have a low bar for compliments if someone saying you're *not* an idiot is your idea of high praise."

"I would take any praise from you, my lady."

I said the words as a joke, but as soon as they left my lips, the truth of them sliced through me. I might not like Asterin, and I definitely didn't trust her, but I respected her. The Erzton lady was smart, strong, and cool under pressure. All admirable qualities, but it was her secrets that intrigued me the most.

How did she slip into Jorge's lab? Had she been playing the corporate-espionage game and hoping to steal some proprietary tech to deliver to her parents? Or did Asterin have her own agenda, independent from her Erzton responsibilities and commitments?

I had always loved a good puzzle—and especially the satisfaction that came from figuring out a particularly complicated one—and I had a feeling that Asterin would be the most challenging problem I had ever attempted to solve.

"You're different from what I thought you would be," Asterin said.

I arched an eyebrow. "Different good or different bad?"

Another thoughtful look filled her face. "Too soon to tell."

"Well, you're also different from what I thought you would be," I countered.

"How so?"

"For starters, I didn't think you would be a spy—or that you would break into Jorge's lab tonight. Care to tell me what you were doing in there? What you were hoping to find or steal?" Asterin crossed her arms over her chest. "Perhaps I was wrong before. Perhaps you are an idiot after all. You certainly have the most ridiculous ideas. Me? A spy? A thief? Hardly."

"Deny it all you want, but only a thief would break into an R&D lab in the middle of a solstice party." I gestured at the blaster still in her hand. "And only a spy would smuggle a pocket-size weapon into a Regal ball."

She huffed, but she quickly slid the blaster into her gown pocket. Then she jerked her chin at my hand. "Says the man carrying a stormsword."

"Touché." I tipped my head to her, then slid my sword into the slot on my weapons belt.

We stared at each other. Asterin's black hair was a tangled mess, her silver eye shadow and liner were severely smudged, and her gray gown was ripped and torn in a dozen places. But somehow she was even lovelier now than she had been on the dance floor, and I found myself easing toward her, like a high tide inevitably drawn to a moonlit shore . . .

"Asterin! Lady Asterin!" a voice bellowed.

I stopped and looked in that direction. Lights appeared in the distance, bobbing back and forth along the edge of the lawn.

Asterin let out another tired sigh. "That's Rigel. He must be worried sick."

"Of course," I murmured. "We should return to the castle. I need to check on my father and my grandmother, as well as everyone else."

Asterin nodded, then strode toward the trees.

I watched her go, feeling as though something monumental had shifted between us. I wasn't quite sure what it was, but somehow I was certain that it was only going to cause me more trouble in the end.

NINE

ZANE

e left the Techwave blitzer behind and made our way back through the woods, along the lakeshore, and up to the lawn.

Rigel was there, clutching a blaster, a hoverglobe bobbing up and down over his right shoulder like a flying flashlight. He rushed over to us. "Asterin! Are you injured?"

"I'm fine," she said, waving him away the same way she had done to me earlier. "Just a few bumps and bruises. I hardly noticed them."

My gaze strayed to the reddish bruise on the side of her head. I didn't see how she didn't notice that, especially given the way the goose egg on my own head was still pounding, but I kept quiet.

Beatrice, Wendell, and Fergus crossed the lawn and stopped, hovering beside Rigel. My gaze roamed over my grandmother, my father, and my friend, but other than their rumpled clothes and dirty, sweaty faces, they looked fine. A tight knot of tension unwound in my chest.

Rigel spun around to me, his eyes burning like brown suns in his tight, angry face. "How did you let this happen, Lord Zane? I thought you were supposed to be the leader of the Arrows. One of the strongest psions and best warriors in all the Imperium. If you can't protect Asterin and keep her from getting kidnapped during a simple celebration, then we need to seriously rethink our potential alliance with the Zimmer family."

My grandmother sucked in a breath and opened her mouth, but my father laid a warning hand on her arm, and she reluctantly remained quiet.

Equal parts hope and annoyance spurted through me at Rigel's harsh words, but my annoyance quickly won out, the way it usually did. "Are you insinuating it's *my* fault that the Techwave attacked the solstice celebration?"

Rigel's continued glower was answer enough, but even more worrisome was the soft chime of confirmation that rippled through my mind at my own words. My psion power was muttering that there was a nugget of truth in my flippant statement. The Techwave might have come here to steal House Rojillo technology, but the attack also had something to do with *me*.

"Tonight's events are the fault of the Techwave, no one else," Beatrice piped up in a sharp tone. "We all know how dangerous they are and that they will do anything to get what they want, even attack a peaceful celebration."

Rigel crossed his arms over his muscled chest. "And what *did* they want, exactly?"

"To be determined," I replied in an icy voice. "But as you so succinctly pointed out, I am the head of the Arrows, which means I have a job to do."

Rigel glowered at me again, but I ignored him and turned to Asterin. Her face was calm, but her shoulders were tense, and her fingers were fisted in her skirt. Now that the threat from the

Techwave was over, she was probably worried that I was going to reveal her extracurricular activities in the R&D lab.

An Erzton lady stealing from a Regal lord would cause *quite* the scandal and would severely damage Asterin's chances of landing a husband, if not destroy her family's quest for an Imperium alliance altogether. No Regal House would want a thief and a spy in their midst. Even my grandmother would think twice about such an arrangement.

Oh, yes, if I revealed Asterin's secret, I could probably end our potential engagement before it even began, but I was going to keep her lab break-in to myself. I would use the information if—and when—it best benefited me. Now was not that time, but future blackmail was always an excellent option.

"Lady Asterin, please excuse me. I must make sure there is no threat of another attack, but I'll check on you again as soon as I can."

Her shoulders relaxed, and her fingers released their white-knuckle grip, although she still eyed me with suspicion. She was right to be wary of my seeming benevolence.

"Of course," she murmured. "Thank you, Lord Zane."

I bowed to Asterin, then straightened up and tipped my head to Rigel, Beatrice, Wendell, and Fergus. I looked at Asterin a heartbeat longer, then spun around on my heel and stalked away to assess just how much damage the Techwave had done.

Despite the destruction on the lawn, no one had been killed, although several guards had been badly burned from the electrical shocks they'd received. The lack of casualties did little to ease my guilt, though. Over the past several months, the Techwave had hit dozens of Regal facilities on various planets, but this attack had happened on *my* watch, while *I* was the head of the Arrows, and innocent people had been hurt and terrorized right under my nose.

Rigel was right about one thing. I hadn't protected Asterin or my family or anyone else tonight. No, tonight I was nothing but a bloody *failure*.

As much as I wanted to slink off into the dark and brood about my many shortcomings, I had work to do, so I packed all my feelings into another permaglass box in my mind and buried it right beside the one still containing all my physical pain. Compartmentalizing my emotions was something else I excelled at as an Arrow.

I spent the next hour moving from one group of Regals, servants, and guards to the next, making sure the injured were treated and the castle was secured. I didn't think the Techwave would return, since they seemed to have gotten exactly what they were after, but I wanted to be prepared in case I was wrong.

Once everyone on the lawn had been taken care of, I went in search of Lord Jorge. I found him and my father in the castle, peering at the destruction inside the bombed-out library.

Jorge's face was gray with shock, and sweat beaded on his forehead, despite the temperature-shielding device on his wrist. "This is my fault," he mumbled in a low, shaky voice, staring at the splintered furniture and charred books. "I was so very *proud* of everything I've accomplished, and I wanted everyone to see how strong House Rojillo is. I never *dreamed* the Techwave would attack the castle, especially during the solstice celebration."

He turned to me, a stricken look on his face. Nausea surged off him and churned in my own stomach. "You were right, Zane. I should have been more careful. I should have implemented your security suggestions. Maybe if I had, none of this would have happened."

Wendell laid a comforting hand on Jorge's shoulder, but I

remained stiff and silent. Jorge was right. If he had implemented my suggestions, we might have thwarted the Techwave attack instead of being left picking up the pieces.

Jorge shuddered out a breath. Then he shrugged off my father's hand, wiped the sweat off his forehead, and straightened his spine. "I will take full responsibility for this disaster with Callus Holloway, the other Regals, and the gossipcasts. You have my word, Zane."

The regret and sincerity in his voice loosened some of the throbbing knots of anger and frustration in my chest. "There will be plenty of time to talk about that later," I said in a rough voice. "Right now, I want to know what the Techwave stole."

I told Jorge and Wendell how Silas had infiltrated the castle, taken Asterin hostage, and accessed the secret library terminal. The only thing I didn't mention was that Asterin had infiltrated the main R&D lab. I wanted to pinpoint what, if anything, she had stolen first. Then I would decide what to do with the information.

Jorge's dark gaze flicked over to the spot where the hidden terminal had been. A grim look filled his face, and he spun around and stalked away. My father and I followed him.

The Regal lord quickly moved from one corridor to the next and went down some steps. Eventually, he ended up in the same R&D lab where I had discovered Asterin earlier. The door was still open, and Jorge stopped and gaped at the terminals, tools, folders, plastipapers, gelpens, and other debris that littered the floor. I hid a grimace. I'd made quite a mess sliding over the workstations when I'd been chasing after Asterin earlier.

"Did the Techwavers access this lab along with my library?" Jorge asked.

"Looks that way," I lied in a calm, steady voice. "Can you tell if they took anything?"

Jorge marched over to a locker in the back of the room and submitted to a series of retinal, DNA, and fingerprint scans.

The grate slid aside, and he yanked out a high table with a holo-screen embedded in the center of the chrome.

Jorge started typing, his fingers flying over the screen. Several holograms appeared, and he swiped them away one at a time. "Looks like the Techies pulled up the designs for House Rojillo's latest air purifier. It's a minor project that's already been on the market for several months. They only looked at it for a few seconds. They must have accessed it by mistake."

He shrugged off the seeming coincidence, but I peered at the time stamp on the last hologram. Not the Techwave—Asterin. Somehow she had gotten past all the lab's security measures and into the House Rojillo servers. I frowned. But what could she possibly want with designs for an air purifier?

Jorge started typing again. After several seconds, his fingers stilled, and a single hologram hovered over the table. "The Techwavers downloaded the schematics for my new tempera-ture-shielding device." His face creased with confusion. "How strange."

"Isn't the technology valuable?" I asked. "You said earlier that you were going to use it to bid on the climate-control con-tracts at Promenade Park."

Jorge shrugged again. "Yes and no. The tech could help me win the contracts, but I don't understand why the Techwave would want it. According to the gossipcast reports, the Techies usually steal weapons, or designs for weapons, or materials to make weapons. Not climate-control tech."

He rubbed the holoscreen on his wristwatch, making it flicker and flare with light. After a few seconds, his fingers stilled, and his shoulders sagged. "It doesn't really matter what the Techwave wants with my designs. No one will give House Rojillo a contract or want to buy our products now. Not after tonight. I'm ruined, and my House and family along with me."

Jorge's gaze dropped to the watch again. An angry snarl spewed from his lips, and he tore the device off his wrist and hurled it across the room as if he couldn't even stand to look at it right now. The device tinked off a wall and dropped to the floor.

Once again, my father laid a sympathetic hand on the other man's shoulder. "The attack wasn't your fault, Jorge. The Techwavers are vicious, determined terrorists who delight in torturing others. They would have gotten what they wanted one way or another. At least no one was killed."

Jorge nodded, but disbelief filled his face. We all knew exactly how quick the Regals were to blame one another for the smallest infraction—and this was *far* from a small infraction.

The other Regals would openly shun the members of House Rojillo, along with their products and services, while the gossipcasts would rip Jorge's reputation to shreds. As for Callus Holloway, well, there was no telling what kind of punishment he might inflict on Jorge personally or what sanctions he might slap on House Rojillo.

Jorge was right. Tonight's attack was exactly the kind of scandal that could destroy a Regal House.

"House Zimmer will stand with you," Wendell said. "Perhaps we can work on your temperature-shielding technology together. Figure out why the Techwave stole it and what they plan to do with it. Perhaps we can even find some way to improve the tech and make it valuable enough that the other Regals can't help but buy it, along with your other products."

Jorge nodded again, but lines of worry, fear, and doubt cut deep grooves into his face, making him look a decade older.

"Come on," my father said in a gentle voice. "There's nothing more you can do in this lab tonight. The workers can help you clean up the mess in the morning."

Jorge gave an absent nod, then shoved the table back into its slot and locked the grate. Wendell steered the other lord out of the R&D lab.

I started to follow them, but then a thought occurred to me, and I headed to the opposite side of the room. I crouched down and grabbed the climate-control device that Jorge had ripped off his wrist.

Despite being thrown against the wall, the device was still in one piece. Wide silver band, a small holoscreen, tiny bits of lunarium and sapphsidian glinting here and there. Once again, it reminded me of an old-fashioned wristwatch instead of the advanced technology it truly was.

I twirled the device back and forth in my fingers, wondering why the Techwave had gone to so much trouble to steal something so small and seemingly harmless—and what deadly thing they were planning to do with it.

TEN

ZANE

J orge posted a few guards outside the R&D lab, but the spaceship was already out of the docking slot, as the old saying went, and it was nothing but a futile show—

Ding! The familiar shrill whistle sounded from my tablet.

Communications in and around the castle had been restored quite some time ago, and I was surprised it had taken Holloway this long to message me. Given the attack, I had no choice but to see what he wanted, so I pulled the device out of my pocket and read the message.

Handle this. Now.

Holloway's short missive included a link to *Celestial Stars*, one of the most popular gossipcasts in the galaxy. Several Regals had already contacted Artemis Swallow, the gossipcast's head producer, to give their eyewitness accounts of the disastrous solstice celebration. I bit back a groan.

"Something wrong?" my father asked.

I slid my tablet back into my pocket. "Time for me to face the gossipcasters. Holloway wants me to spin the story."

Jorge nodded and straightened his spine again. "Then we will face them—together."

My father returned to the lawn while Jorge and I made our way to the front of the castle. An army of gossipcasters were camped outside, dozens more than those who had originally been here covering the solstice celebration, all of them breathlessly reporting about the Techwave attack. I ground my teeth. The gossipcasts were a useful tool, but at times like these, I wanted to drive my stormsword into every last camera and microphone.

Jorge flinched, but he yanked down his tailcoat, girding himself for battle. I unclenched my jaw and did the same thing. Jorge nodded at me, and together the two of us stepped out of the castle and stopped in the designated media space. Had it only been a few hours since I'd last been here talking about my shampoo commercial? Right now, it seemed like days.

The gossipcasters surged forward, yelling questions and jostling for position behind the pink velvet ropes.

"Zane! Lord Zane! Who was the target of tonight's attack?"

"Was anything stolen? Was anyone killed?"

"How will you guarantee the Regals' safety moving forward?"

I would rather face down an entire squad of Black Scarabs single-handedly than endure this media gauntlet right now, but I didn't have a choice, so I fixed a calm, reassuring smile on my face and looked directly into the bright glare of the cameras.

I needed to do at least one bloody thing right tonight.

For the next fifteen minutes, I answered one question after another. I kept my voice steady and my answers vague and simple and projected as much confidence as I could muster. Everything was under control, the intruders had been killed, the other Arrows were already hot on the trail of the masterminds, and the Techwave wouldn't dare to attack Corios again on my watch.

Lies, all of it.

"Is it true Lord Jorge ignored the Arrows' security sugges-tions?" a gossipcaster yelled out. "That his oversight allowed the Techwavers to attack unimpeded? That his carelessness is the primary cause for tonight's calamity?"

Beside me, Jorge's face paled. His stomach gurgled with ominous notes, but he drew in a breath and stepped forward. "I must take—"

"I must take severe umbrage at those insinuations," I smoothly cut in. "Lord Jorge followed all Imperium security suggestions to the letter. Nothing more could have been done by him or House Rojillo to prevent tonight's attack."

I stepped forward, putting myself between Jorge and the bright glares of the cameras. "Rest assured that we have learned a great deal from tonight's attack. Why, the Arrows are already making use of all the information we've collected, just as we intended."

The gossipcasters frowned. Several of them glanced at one another, then back at me.

"Just as you intended? What does that mean?"

"What information? Did the Techwave leave some sort of data or device behind?"

"Will tonight's attack somehow lead the Arrows to a Tech-wave base? Or all the Regal weapons and resources the terrorist group has stolen in recent months?"

"I'm not at liberty to reveal specifics on Arrow missions, targets, or objectives." I flashed them all another smile, then gave an exaggerated wink. "But believe me when I say that Corios is safer than ever, and we can all sleep peacefully to-night."

Once again, the gossipcasters frowned and glanced at one another, not sure what to make of my confusing, contradictory statements, but that was the point. The more I clouded the truth and downplayed what had happened tonight, the more the gossipcasters would speculate and talk in useless circles.

Disinformation was a weapon too, and I wasn't just wielding it because of Holloway's orders. I didn't want to embolden General Orion Ocnus and the other mysterious leaders of the Techwave or give them any tactical advantages by revealing how chaotic and successful their attack had been and just how close they'd come to killing the solstice guests. Of course, the Regals who had already given interviews about their harrowing experiences would undercut my strategy, but I'd spun the story the best I could.

The gossipcasters sucked in a collective breath to pepper me with more questions, but I smiled, waved, and ended the press conference. The gossipcasters started yelling again, but I ignored them and escorted Lord Jorge back inside the castle. I shut a door behind us, finally, mercifully, cutting off the barrage of questions.

Jorge slumped against the wall, looking as tired as I felt. "Thank you for that," he said in a low, strained voice. "For saying my security was excellent and that no one could have prevented the Techwave attack."

I shrugged off his thanks. "It was nothing."

Jorge stepped forward and clasped my hand in his own. "Not to me. Perhaps my House will survive this disaster after all."

Tears gleamed in his eyes, but he blinked them back, dropped my hand, and cleared his throat. "Please excuse me. I want to see how everyone is doing. I also need to make arrangements for the guests to either spend the night here or return home, whichever they prefer."

"Of course," I murmured. "Please let me know if I can be of any assistance."

Jorge gave me a wan smile and disappeared deeper into the castle. I scrubbed my hands through my hair, trying to slough off everything that had happened over the past few hours. Then I went in search of my family.

Fergus had vanished, probably to check on the rest of the House Zimmer servants and escort them home, but Beatrice and Wendell were still out on the lawn, along with several of the Regals. I looked them over for a second time, but other than their disheveled appearances, they were fine.

Relief rushed through me. I didn't know what I would have done if I had lost them, and yet I couldn't help but feel like that had been someone's goal tonight, given the way the Black Scarab had seemed to search for and then specifically target my father.

As for who would want to hurt my family, well, it was a long, long list. You didn't get to be among the most powerful Regal Houses by playing nicely with others, and my grandmother had made plenty of enemies over the years with her various schemes. I'd made my fair share of enemies too, both as a Regal lord and especially as an Arrow.

And then, of course, there was Vesper. Perhaps I was being paranoid, but I felt like tonight's attack also had something to do with *her*. My surprise sister hadn't been a Regal long, but she had enemies too, especially since she kept foiling the Techwave's plots. Either way, a faint unease kept thrumming through my body, and my psionic instincts kept whispering that this wasn't the end of my family's battle with the Techwave— more like the beginning.

"Zane? Are you okay?" my father asked. "You have a strange look on your face."

I shook off my thoughts of Vesper and the Techwave. "I'm all right. I just wanted to double-check on the two of you."

My grandmother waved her hand. "We're fine, thanks to you and your father."

I grinned at him. "Nice trick with the string of bulbs and the fork. I didn't realize you could make solar lights explode like that."

An answering grin creased Wendell's face, although it

quickly morphed into a thoughtful look. "My trick would have been better if it had blown the Scarab completely apart like I intended. I've never been particularly good at thinking of solutions on the fly and under pressure. Not like other people. Why, I bet—"

He cut off his words, but a wave of wistfulness washed off him, and the rest of his thought echoed through my mind: *Vesper would have made it work.*

A cold fist wrapped around my heart and squeezed it tight. My father didn't even know his daughter, not really, but he already had the utmost confidence in her abilities, just as he'd always had the same unwavering faith in mine.

"What about Lady Asterin?" my grandmother asked. "Were you able to give her the solstice gift before the attack?"

I suppressed a sigh. No matter the situation, Beatrice always focused on business first and foremost, something I admired and despised about her in equal measure. "No, I didn't give her the gift earlier, and I don't see the point of giving it to her now. You heard what Rigel said about Asterin's family rethinking their alliance with House Zimmer in the wake of my great and terrible incompetence as an Arrow tonight."

My grandmother huffed, the sound full of scathing derision. "As if the Erzton Hammers would have done any better if they had been here. I'll speak to Rigel and make sure he and the Colliers understand how foolish it would be to stop our negotiations."

She speared me with a sharp look. "Find Asterin, give her the solstice gift, and smooth things over the best you can. Understand, Zane?"

I suppressed another sigh, too tired to argue with her right now. "Yes, Beatrice."

My grandmother made a shooing motion with her hand. "There is no time like the present. Perhaps we can salvage something out of this dreadful evening."

"As always, your wish is my command," I drawled.

Beatrice sniffed, not appreciating my mocking compliance, but she moved over to a group of Regals and started talking to them. My father gave me an apologetic smile, then did the same thing, going over to some of his friends.

I scanned the lawn, but Asterin wasn't here, so I went inside the castle in search of the Erzton lady.

By this point, it was after midnight, which meant the summer solstice was officially over. Many of the Regals had gone inside the castle to find their rooms for the night or to wait for transports to take them home, but I didn't see Asterin in any of the sitting areas.

I moved from one room and corridor to the next, smiling and nodding at everyone I passed, although I received angry glowers and muttered curses in return. A few folks stepped forward and stabbed their fingers at me, but I kept moving. I'd already talked enough to the gossipcasters, and I had no desire to endure any more pointed questions and stinging reprimands about my failures. I wanted some more skinbonds, a hot shower, and a soothing cup of tea, not necessarily in that order, but I'd be lucky if I got any of those things before sunrise.

Eventually, I stuck my head into a conservatory. More pink-star honeysuckles curled through the enormous room, perfuming the air with their sweet scent, while the permaglass dome overhead revealed the full breadth and beauty of the night sky, as though a black velvet blanket studded with white sequin stars had been draped over this part of the castle.

Low whispers of conversation caught my ear. I was never shy about eavesdropping, so I slipped into the conservatory, moving from one honeysuckle-lined path to another until I reached the center of the round room. Up ahead, three people were huddled on chaise lounges and having an intense discusion—Tivona Winslow, Leandra Ferrum, and Asterin Armas.

My steps were silent, but Asterin looked in my direction as if she could sense my presence some other way. Strange. I was usually much better at sneaking up on people, but she'd caught me spying, and all I could do now was own it.

The three women shot to their feet, and I plastered a smile on my face and swaggered over to them.

"Ladies! Just wanted to check and make sure you weren't suffering any ill effects from the evening's events."

Tivona slapped her hands on her hips. "What did you expect? That we'd be swooning on the settees, and you would have to fetch us some smelling salts?"

I grinned at her. "I'm always happy to fetch smelling salts or anything else you require."

Tivona huffed and rolled her eyes. "You are impossible, just like—"

Vesper. She bit off her thought, but it whispered through my mind anyway.

Once again, a cold fist squeezed my heart, but I kept my smile fixed on my face. I raised my eyebrows in a silent question, but Tivona shook her head.

"Nothing," she muttered. "Never mind."

When it became apparent Tivona wasn't going to say anything else, I turned to Leandra. "You were extremely impressive tonight. You cut through those Scarabs like you were pruning weeds in a garden. What would it take to convince you to join the Arrows?"

Leandra let out a low, amused laugh. "You couldn't afford my price, Zane."

"Which would be what, exactly? I am not without resources. Neither is Callus Holloway. The Imperium royal coffers are quite substantial. Why, they are practically *bursting* with credits. I'm sure we could come to some mutually beneficial arrangement."

She rolled her eyes. "By the stars, you are persistent."

My smile widened. "It's one of my best traits and many charms."

Asterin snorted, although it sounded suspiciously close to a laugh. At least I was amusing someone tonight.

"Well, I need a drink to deal with your supposed *charms*," Leandra sniped.

"I assure you, my offer is quite genuine. I could use someone like you in the Arrows."

Leandra laughed again, then shook her head and walked away. Tivona shot me another angry glower and followed her, leaving me alone with Asterin.

I looked her over the same way I had done with Beatrice and Wendell earlier. Someone, most likely Rigel, must have given her a skinbond, because the reddish bruise on the side of her head had vanished, as had the cuts, scrapes, and other minor injuries that had dotted her skin.

Asterin crossed her arms over her chest. "What do you want, Zane? It's been a long night. I want to go to my hotel, soak in a warm bath, and go to bed."

She wasn't the only one who was exhausted, but I still had one final duty to perform, so I reached into my coat pocket and drew out the lunarium jewelry box I'd been carrying around for hours.

Asterin froze. Something that looked a lot like panic flickered across her face, although the emotion vanished in an instant. "What is *that*?" she asked in a sharp, suspicious voice.

I turned the box around in my hands. The Techwave cannon blast had melted the delicate silver filigree, transforming the once-elegant ribbons into jagged bumps of metal. Most of the pale lunarium still sparkled with color, although the edges were as charred and blackened as my ruined tailcoat. "It was a solstice gift for you, although I'm afraid it got damaged when Silas blasted me in the chest."

Asterin's eyebrows shot up. "That box saved you from the Techwaver's cannon?"

"More or less."

I dug my fingers into the silver seams, which had fused together. It took me several tries, along with a fair bit of telekinesis, but I finally managed to pry the box open.

The lunarium might have saved my life, but the entire box had overheated and melted the necklace inside. The silver choker studded with blue opals was now a lumpy mass of metal and jewels that looked like it had been fused together without any true purpose, beauty, or design.

I grimaced. "I'm sorry. I was hoping the necklace might have survived the cannon blast. I could have it repaired . . ." My voice trailed off. We could both see there was no saving the necklace.

"There's no need for that. It's the thought that counts, right?" Asterin gave me a tired smile that didn't even come close to reaching her eyes.

"I suppose so," I replied, matching her forced politeness. "Perhaps I can give you a proper gift the next time we meet."

Asterin shook her head. "That's not necessary." Her lips twisted. "Besides, I've just received an urgent message. My mother and stepfather would like me to return home for a while, given what happened here tonight."

I slowly closed the box and dropped it to my side. "I see."

Asterin going back to her home planet of Sygnustern meant that we wouldn't be getting engaged anytime soon. In fact, Asterin's departure might just spell the end of my grandmother's marriage scheme once and for all. I should be happy, ecstatic, thrilled, even. But instead, I felt . . . unsettled. Then again, I always felt better when I could keep an eye on my enemies—and Asterin *was* an enemy.

Oh, she might not try to murder me outright or be actively plotting the downfall of the Imperium like the Techwave was, but it was clear that Asterin Armas had her own agenda. I had enough problems of my own to solve. I didn't need to get entangled in anyone else's complications, but I had the strangest sense that I was going to get dragged into Asterin's mysterious troubles sooner rather than later.

"Thank you for coming after me when the Black Scarab dragged me into the woods," Asterin said in a stiff voice, as if it physically pained her to say the words.

I wouldn't have wanted to thank me either, and it would have greatly annoyed me to have to say the words to her if our roles had been reversed. I had never enjoyed having to make nice with an adversary, even when we were briefly on the same side.

Asterin cleared her throat. "You didn't have to do that," she finished.

"Yes, I did."

I would have helped Asterin no matter what kind of danger she was in, because that was my job as an Arrow. It might not be much, but it was the only bit of honor I had. Besides, Asterin was the most intriguing person I had met in a long time. Intriguing people might make life difficult, but they also made it interesting. I'd much rather triumph in a hard-fought battle over a worthy opponent than steamroll over a weak enemy, and Asterin Armas was definitely *not* weak.

Asterin hesitated, and when she spoke again, her voice was pitched much lower and softer than before. "I hope you find the answers you're looking for, especially about Vesper and the rest of your family."

My chest tightened, but I forced myself to smile as though her words didn't bother me at all. "Thank you." I cleared my throat, remembering what she had revealed to me on the dance floor. "And good luck with your family as well."

She smiled back at me, her expression as tight and tense as mine. "Good-bye, Zane."

"Good-bye, Asterin."

She studied me a second longer, then spun around and strode away.

Tivona and Leandra were waiting for Asterin at the front of the conservatory. The three women put their heads together and started whispering in low voices again. Their conspiratorial coven reminded me of how the three of them had worked together during the midnight ball, along with Daichi and Touma Hirano, to help Kyrion and Vesper escape from Crownpoint.

When I'd first arrived at Castle Rojillo, I'd quipped to the gossipcasters that none of the Regals would help Kyrion Caldaren. I was absolutely right about that. Kyrion didn't have any real friends among the Regals. Even if he did, none of the lords and ladies would risk helping him for fear of incurring Holloway's wrath. Neither would any of the Arrows. There was no place on any Imperium-controlled planet that Kyrion could hide where I wouldn't find him within a matter of weeks.

But I had overlooked the other half of this fugitive equation or, in this case, the other half of Kyrion's truebond: Vesper. Because my sister *did* have friends—true friends who would do anything for her, even shelter her from the Imperium.

And chief among those friends was Asterin Armas.

Vesper and Kyrion had helped Asterin protect her people and property on Tropics 33 during the recent Techwave attack there. Given her earlier talk of honor, I had no doubt the Erzton lady thought she owed the couple a debt, and there was one obvious way she could repay it. Of course. I should have seen it sooner. Perhaps I would have seen it sooner if I hadn't been so focused on my own issues with Asterin.

I didn't need the Imperium's generals or the Arrows' information or even my own network of spies. I knew *exactly* where Kyrion and Vesper were going and where they planned to hide from Holloway while they figured out their next move—Sygnustern, the Erzton home planet.

But the knowledge didn't fill me with the sense of triumph I'd expected. Instead, a surprising amount of worry gnawed at my heart, while a nagging question whispered through my mind.

What was I going to do with the information?

ELEVEN

ZANE

I left the conservatory and did another lap through the castle, checking on everyone and making sure the structure was secured, along with the surrounding grounds. I also gave some final instructions to the House Rojillo guards, along with the Imperium soldiers, investigators, engineers, and scientists who had arrived to examine the Techwave ship. Finally, around three in the morning, I got into the House Zimmer carriage with my father and my grandmother, and we returned to the spaceport and took a private transport back to the city.

It was creeping up on sunrise when we stepped into my grandmother's library in Castle Zimmer. Several servants were waiting to see if we needed anything, including Fergus. I asked one of the servants to take Silas's tablet to my tower library, along with his hand cannon. I wanted to examine both devices before I turned them over to my father, and eventually, the Imperium investigators.

Once that was done, Beatrice told everyone to get some rest and dismissed the servants.

Fergus stopped beside me and eyed the scorched fabric on my chest. "Are you really okay, Zane?"

"Right as acid rain," I chirped. "Although I am very sorry about the tailcoat. I know how long and hard you worked on it."

Fergus waved his hand. "I never get attached to any of my designs. Clothes are made to be worn, enjoyed, and admired. And even destroyed on occasion." A sly, teasing grin crept across the tailor's face. "Although no one destroys clothes quite as spectacularly as you do, my lord."

I snorted. "I'm glad one of us can joke about this."

Fergus's grin grew a little wider. He clapped me on the shoulder, then left the library, shutting the doors behind him.

"What a bloody night," my grandmother muttered, pouring herself a hefty snifter of strawberry brandy.

She tossed the brandy back in one long gulp, then refilled her snifter. She offered some to my father and me, but we both declined. Beatrice went over and sat down in the chair behind her desk. Despite the long night and the trying events of the solstice celebration, her posture remained ramrod straight as always. I admired her stamina, even as I sprawled across one of the overstuffed settees, digging the toes of my boots into the floor to keep from sliding off the slick cushions.

My father let out a weary sigh and eased down into a chair across from me. "Have you learned anything more about the Techwave attack? Or what they might be plotting to do with Jorge's temperature-shielding technology?"

"Not yet. Although Holloway sent me a message earlier that was short and sweet and practically dripping with fury."

Beatrice snorted. "You mean Holloway is furious about how the attack is playing out on the gossipcasts. How many Regals are openly questioning his leadership and blaming him because the Techwavers haven't been neutralized yet."

I slumped a little deeper into the cushions, too tired to even agree with her. Holloway put on a good show for the gossip-casts, but we all knew that he only cared about himself.

After ordering me to spin the story, the Imperium leader hadn't contacted me since then. No doubt he was too busy trying to reassure the more important, demanding Regals that everything was under control to bother with threatening me, although I was sure that would change soon enough. But for now, I would enjoy the relative quiet.

I looked at my father. "What could the Techwave do with Lord Jorge's stolen tech? You saw the schematics. Is the design as promising as he seemed to think?"

Jorge's temperature-shielding wristwatch was nestled in my pocket, right next to the jewelry box I was still carrying around like a lumpy, melted albatross. I didn't mention the watch, though. My father would chastise me for taking it, and I had no desire to listen to a lecture right now. Besides, I had a strange feeling that Jorge's watch was one of the keys to the Techwave's ultimate plot, whatever it was, and I wanted to glean as much information from the device as possible.

My father spread his hands out wide. "It's hard to say without studying the schematics in greater detail, but Jorge has been bragging about his climate-control technology for months to anyone who would listen. If he's really come up with some sort of breakthrough, then the Techwave could use it in numerous ways. They might even be able to weaponize the technology in some way."

More weariness crashed over me. The Techwave was already developing weapons to use against the Arrows and other powerful psions, and this theft was just another nail in what the terrorist group wanted to be the collective coffin of the Imperium.

My father fell silent, while my grandmother continued to drink her brandy. My gaze strayed up to the portrait of Miriol on the wall. Had it only been a few hours since my father and

I had been looking at my mother's picture? It seemed like a lifetime.

I glanced back and forth between my father and my grandmother, and anger spurted through me, burning away my weariness. I had been waiting for them to reveal the truth about Vesper for the last two weeks, but they had remained silent, and they would continue to remain silent—unless I dragged this unexpected family secret out into the light.

I straightened up on the settee and put my feet on the floor. I studied my father and my grandmother, plotting the best method of attack. Then I cleared my throat, drawing their attention. "There's something else. I'll be leaving soon. Perhaps in a day or two."

Beatrice frowned at me over the rim of her brandy snifter. "To go where and do what?"

"Hunt down Kyrion Caldaren and Vesper Quill," I replied in a calm, even voice. "I've finally figured out where they're hiding. Or at least where they are going to hide."

My father tensed. "What will you do once you find them?"

I shrugged. "Exactly what Holloway has ordered: drag them both back to Corios. Given tonight's attack, Holloway will be even more eager and desperate to take their truebond power so he can shore up his rule."

Wendell glanced over at Beatrice, whose fingers tightened around her brandy snifter. She shook her head the tiniest bit in warning. My father's jaw clenched, and his hands curled into fists.

More anger flooded my chest. They were still clinging to their stubborn silence. Well, the time for secrets was over. Now it was time for us all to face some hard truths.

"I'll concentrate my efforts on Vesper," I continued in a light, breezy tone. "She will be much easier to subdue than Kyrion. I captured her before on Tropics 33, and I have no doubt I can do it again."

"Holloway wants Vesper brought back to Corios unharmed, yes?" my father asked, an apprehensive note creeping into his voice.

I laughed, but it was a low, ugly, mocking sound. "Of course not. Holloway told me to do whatever is necessary to separate Vesper from Kyrion. Holloway doesn't care what shape Vesper is in when I dump her at his feet, just that she's alive enough for him to siphon off her power."

I gave my father a careless shrug. "I'll probably have to chop off a few of her fingers, maybe even a toe or two, to break her spirit, but sooner or later, Vesper will do whatever Holloway wants. She'll quickly become his living, breathing battery. So will Kyrion, just like Desdemona and Chauncey Caldaren before them."

My father jerked upright in his chair, and all the color drained from his face. "No! No, Zane, you can't do that! You can't hurt Vesper!"

"Why not? Vesper Quill is just some little lab rat who lucked into being a Regal lady." I gave him another careless shrug. "No one important enough to care about."

My father recoiled as if I was some horrific monster he had never seen before. Wendell might know I was an Arrow, might know about all the horrific things I did to please Holloway and help maintain House Zimmer's exalted status, but to him, the battles and killings and assassinations were abstract theories. Whereas to me, they were only cruel choices and the evil constants that shaped my existence.

"Zane is right," Beatrice said in a cool, measured voice. "Vesper Quill is no one important, and she won't escape Holloway's clutches, no matter how powerful her truebond is with Kyrion Caldaren."

My father jerked in his chair again, and his mouth gaped as he looked at my grandmother. Beatrice shook her head again, a clear warning to stay quiet. My father's mouth snapped shut, and an angry red flush zoomed up his neck and stained his cheeks, but he remained stiff and silent in his chair.

Something cracked open deep inside my chest, and a laugh burst out of my mouth, like water spurting through a broken dam. Then another one . . . then another one . . .

My father and my grandmother both frowned, clearly confused, but I couldn't stop my loud, harsh, mirthless cackles, even though they made my ribs ache and brought tears to my eyes.

Finally, all the laughter had escaped, although a cold, bitter sensation flooded my chest in the empty space that was left behind.

I looked at my grandmother. "I've watched you plot and scheme and manipulate people my entire life. And I've endured your plots, schemes, and manipulations myself, including your attempts to force me into a relationship with Lady Asterin, all so you—and by extension House Zimmer—can get your hands on the mineral rights she controls. But . . ." My voice trailed off, and I shook my head.

"But what?" Beatrice asked in the tense, charged silence.

I stared her in the eyes. "But this is the first time that I've ever been ashamed of you."

Beatrice flinched as though I had slapped her.

I leaned forward and stabbed my finger at her. "My whole life—*my whole bloody life*—you have drilled one thing into my head: Family first, House Zimmer second, then the galaxy could take everyone else. It's practically our family fucking motto, but it's all a lie. You have *never* put family first."

I leaned forward a little more, and when I spoke, my voice and body vibrated with dark fury. "Otherwise, you wouldn't have abandoned your own granddaughter."

Beatrice's lips pinched together, while Wendell sucked in a ragged breath. I kept staring at my grandmother. Her perfect posture slipped, and she slumped down over her desk.

"You know about Vesper?" my grandmother asked in a high, shaky voice.

"That she's my sister? Oh, yes. Kyrion informed me of that pertinent fact right before the midnight ball. And then, of course, we all heard Vesper confront Nerezza Blackwell about being her biological mother."

I swung my furious gaze over to Wendell, who grimaced and shot a guilty look up at Miriol's portrait. "Don't worry, Father. I've done the math. Your affair with Nerezza started *after* my mother died."

His grimace deepened, and regret sparked in my chest. My father hadn't known about Vesper until the night of the Regal ball. For that, he was blameless, although I was still pissed at him for keeping this secret from me for the last few weeks. Then again, I supposed I had done the same thing to him.

"I understand," I said in a softer, gentler voice. "You were grieving Mother's loss, and Nerezza was Nerezza. It's not your fault."

I stabbed my finger at my grandmother again. "It's *her* fault."

Beatrice lifted her chin and straightened up in her chair. "I did what I thought was best for our family. Nothing more, nothing less."

Another harsh laugh erupted from my mouth. "But you did a whole lot *less* for Vesper, didn't you?"

Beatrice glowered at me, her icy eyes glittering with anger. "You have no idea what I've done for Vesper."

Given my own research and the information my sources had uncovered, I had a pretty good idea of the things she'd done, but that didn't matter right now. I surged to my feet. So did Wendell, who glanced back and forth between Beatrice and me. My grandmother remained in her chair, although she sat up even straighter and stiffer than before, as if girding herself for the battle she knew was coming next.

"Tell me, Grandmother. When Vesper revealed that Nerezza was her mother, how desperate were you to keep your bastard granddaughter a secret from the other Regals?" I asked, my voice a low, dangerous snarl. "Would you have let Holloway kill Vesper the night of the Regal ball? Because it sure looked like you weren't going to lift a finger to help her."

"Holloway was never going to kill Vesper or Kyrion," she countered. "His lust for truebonds is too strong. He would have kept them both alive as long as possible, just as he did to the Caldarens. Sooner or later, I would have found some way to help Vesper."

I stabbed my finger at her yet again. "But you knew—*you bloody knew*—that Holloway had sent me to drag Vesper back to Corios. I told you how he siphoned off her magic in the throne room before the midnight ball, and I even gave you the footage from the spy camera hidden in my Arrow jacket. You saw exactly how much Holloway hurt Vesper when he took her psion power, and yet you still said *nothing* about our connection."

Beatrice shook her head. "There were extenuating circumstances. I had my suspicions, but I didn't know who Vesper truly was until after she confronted Nerezza at the midnight ball."

I kept glowering at her. "It doesn't matter when you found out who Vesper really was. You didn't tell me Vesper was part of our *family*, the one thing you've always told me—*ordered me*—to cherish, protect, and defend above all others. Well, you might not have done your job, but I did *mine*."

My father's eyes widened in surprise. "*You* helped them escape. Somehow you helped Vesper and Kyrion get out of the throne room and out of the palace the night of the ball."

"Of course I did," I snarled. "The two of you weren't going to do anything, so I took matters into my own hands."

Beatrice's fingers clenched into fists on top of her desk,

worry creasing her face. "What did you do, Zane?"

"Nothing that can be traced back to me. Vesper's friends did most of the heavy lifting. I just gave her and Kyrion a little push when they needed it most."

I'd given them a literal push. During the throne room fight, I had used a tiny bit of my telekinesis to help Vesper and Kyrion wriggle free of the Imperium soldiers and Bronze Hand guards attacking them so the couple could finally reach each other and unleash their truebond power.

Wendell exhaled a relieved breath and raked his fingers through his hair. More disgust shot through me.

"I might have done a lot of horrible things in my life, Father, but even I draw the line at murdering my own sister."

He flinched again, but I ignored his hurt and turned my attention back to my grandmother.

"Why did you do it?" I demanded. "Why did you keep Vesper's existence a secret all these years?"

"Because Nerezza Blackwell would have used Vesper to sink her claws into your father, into House Zimmer," Beatrice said, a defensive note creeping into her voice. "I couldn't let that happen. Nerezza would have ruined our family."

She drew in a breath, then let it out, along with a rush of words. "Nerezza wouldn't have been satisfied with being Wendell's wife. Sooner or later, she would have moved against us and tried to position herself as the sole head of House Zimmer. Me, your father, even you, Zane. Nerezza would have eliminated us one by one until only she was left. I could see it all playing out so clearly—the deaths of everyone I loved."

That familiar chime rang in my mind, and my power whispered the truth of her worries. My grandmother might have been wrong about everything else, but she had been right about Nerezza. The Regal climber would have eliminated us one by one—and perhaps even Vesper too—in order to take complete control of House Zimmer.

Beatrice shuddered as though the visions still haunted her. Then she straightened up in her chair again, her face as hard as granite. "I couldn't let that happen to our House, and I would not *let* that happen to my family."

"So you sacrificed an innocent child to hold on to your position. Just like Nerezza abandoned Vesper to become a Regal climber." I shook my head, more disgust filling me. "Perhaps you and Nerezza are more alike than you think."

Beatrice's lips pinched together, but she remained silent.

"Vesper is *not* Nerezza," I snapped. "You could have gotten to know her when she came to Corios a few months ago, but you didn't even give her a chance. Well, that was a grave error on your part, because Vesper is *amazing*—smart, strong, capable, and exceptionally clever. And now she has a truebond with Kyrion, which makes her even more dangerous and powerful. Why, Vesper Quill could be the queen of the whole bloody Imperium if she wanted to be."

Once again, that soft, telltale chime sounded in my mind. Vesper Quill, the queen of the Imperium? Now, *that* would be an interesting wrinkle.

"If you didn't know the truth about Vesper, then you would do exactly what Holloway ordered. You would drag Vesper back to Corios, cut off her fingers and toes, shove her in one of the palace medical labs, and not think twice about any of it," Beatrice snapped back at me. "In some ways, you're even more vicious and ruthless than I am, so don't be so damn self-righteous with me, my darling boy."

"Absolutely," I agreed. "But I do know the truth, and unlike you, I'm going to actually *do* something about it."

Wendell looked at me, and the burgeoning hope on his face made another sharp dagger of regret twist in my gut.

"Oh, why do you even care so much?" Beatrice snapped again. "You've been perfectly happy being an only child and the heir to House Zimmer for the last thirty-eight years."

"Because I could have had a sister," I said in a soft, tired voice. "I could have had someone to help me, someone to help shoulder the burden of House Zimmer. I could have had someone else to trust."

I could have had someone else to love.

The thought popped into my mind, and the truth of it sliced straight through my heart. I rubbed my chest, but that didn't banish the dull, hollow ache.

Once again, Beatrice's posture cracked. Her shoulders sagged, and she braced an elbow against her desk, as if she needed its solid support to hold herself upright. Lines of pain and regret grooved into her face, making her look every single one of her eighty-some years. "I just did what I thought was best for everyone."

Her strained, shaky voice added to the ache in my chest.

"I know," I replied, all the heat and anger gone from my own voice. "But you took my sister away from me, and I don't know if I'll ever be able to forgive you for that."

I ignored Beatrice's stricken expression, along with Wendell's, and stalked out of the library.

TWELVE

ZANE

I couldn't deal with any more family drama right now, so I went to my tower library and shut and locked the door behind me.

I stomped around for the better part of a minute, pacing past the piles of books and weapons haphazardly strewn across the tables, but slowly, the rest of my anger drained away, leaving behind an empty, hollow, cracked cavern deep in my chest.

I stopped in front of the mirror I had used to get ready for the solstice celebration. Mussed blond hair, dull blue eyes, dirt and grime streaked across my cheeks, and of course, the black hole in my tailcoat where Silas had shot me with his hand cannon. The Techwaver might not have killed me, but his aim had been truer than he realized, and I didn't feel like I even had a heart right now. No, right now, all I could feel was the aching loss and brimming bitterness in the place where my heart should be.

Another harsh laugh spewed from my lips, and I spun away from the mirror.

My gaze landed on the brewmaker on a nearby table. I should make myself a cup of tea, cram a few protein bars into my mouth, and get cleaned up. Perhaps even take a quick nap, if I could somehow drift off for a few minutes. Holloway would want me to report to Crownpoint and give him all the details about the Techwave attack as soon as the sun was up.

A tired sigh escaped my lips, but I went over to the table. I fished Jorge's wristwatch and Asterin's jewelry box out of my coat pocket and set them aside, then rummaged through the table's center drawer looking for a pod of blueberry tea. The motions reignited the dull ache in my ribs. Another skinbond injector wouldn't hurt either—

A presence stirred the air behind me, and the sweet, soft scent of spearmint flooded the tower library. I froze, then slowly straightened up and turned around.

Vesper was here.

She was standing in the middle of my library, a confused look on her face, as if she didn't know how she had gotten here.

Over the past few weeks, I'd studied countless photos of my sister, so her features were as familiar to me as my own—dark brown hair with a few red highlights, pale skin, and dark blue eyes studded with silver flecks. She was wearing an Arrow uniform of a tactical jacket over a matching shirt, cargo pants, and knee-high boots, all in the sapphsidian blue of House Caldaren.

My lips curled in disgust. Out of all the people in the galaxy, my sister had a truebond with Kyrion bloody Caldaren. I hoped whatever quirk of fate that arranged this vicious irony was having a long, hearty laugh at my expense.

I stepped away from the table. Vesper's startled gaze flew over to me, and her image flickered just a bit around the edges, like a hologram. We faced off in the middle of my library.

"Astral projection?" I drawled. "My, my, my. You must be a

much stronger seer than I realized to do that." I tilted my head to the side. "Or perhaps Kyrion's power is fueling your own and driving it to even greater heights. I don't know much about truebonds."

"Trust me, this little appearance is as surprising to me as it is to you," she muttered.

Vesper crossed her arms over her chest and looked me up and down, her gaze lingering on the hole in my coat, the black ring that marked my heart like a macabre bull's-eye. "Rough night?"

"You could say that." I crossed my arms over my own chest and leaned my left hip back against the table, mimicking her posture. "There was a minor incident with the Techwave."

She snorted. "A squad of Black Scarabs rampaging through a Regal ball is a bit more serious than a minor incident."

"Agree to disagree."

She snorted again. She dropped her arms, then turned around in a slow circle, studying the library. "Your lair is very cluttered."

"Lair? That's a bit harsh."

"All villains have lairs."

"You consider me to be a villain? That stings almost as much as this did." I gestured at the black hole in my coat.

Vesper rolled her eyes. "And yet you're still alive." She frowned and studied my coat a little more closely. "That scorch mark is from a hand cannon. I recognize the burn pattern."

"Not just any hand cannon." I gestured over at Silas's weapon, which was lying on a stack of books on a nearby table, along with his tablet. "*That* cannon."

Recognition flickered across her face, and her frown deepened. "How did you survive a blast from one of the new Techwave hand cannons? They're designed to cut right through psionic shields and kill Arrows like you."

I grinned at her. "Trade secret. Or perhaps I'm just a little tougher, stronger, and smarter than your boy Kyrion."

She rolled her eyes again. "Kyrion is not *my boy*."

"Ah, but you didn't hear him waxing poetic about your many virtues before the midnight ball. He's quite mad for you."

A smile softened Vesper's lips, and her eyes sparkled with warmth. She was as mad about Kyrion as he was about her, which meant I wasn't going to be able to shove my stormsword into the broody bastard's chest after all. Damn. I had been looking forward to that.

Vesper turned around in a slow circle again, her gaze going from one pile of books and weapons to another. "So much clutter."

"Is that a problem?"

"No, it just reminds me . . ."

"Of what?"

She grimaced. "My own workshop at Quill Corp. And my apartment. They're both very cluttered."

I knew they were. After Vesper and Kyrion had escaped from Corios, I'd gone to Quill Corp and her apartment on Temperate 42 to see if she might have left any clues behind, and the clutter had felt strangely, eerily familiar.

"You should see the mess in my father's workshop. Perhaps clutter runs in our family," I drawled.

Vesper jerked, and her eyes locked with mine again. "So you know that I'm your . . . sister."

The word escaped her lips with a hiss, as though it was a bitter poison she was trying to spit out.

I arched an eyebrow. "I might not be the strongest or most skilled telepath, but I can hear the thoughts of others when I want to. Besides, Kyrion was quite clear in the elevator before the midnight ball. He was very smug and dramatic about it, flicking his fingers, showing me the eye carved into his palm, and whispering the words *Vesper Quill is your sister.* Why, he was so bloody smug and dramatic that I wanted to shove my stormsword into his chest. I still do."

Kyrion had been smug because he'd known—*he'd known*—how the information would impact me. Kyrion knew that family meant everything to me and that I would do anything to protect my father and my grandmother . . . and my sister too. The rogue Arrow had been *counting* on it, and his gamble had paid off, since I'd done exactly what he thought I would.

I'd played right into his hands, something that still irked me.

Oh, Kyrion might not realize all the things I'd done to help him and Vesper escape. How I'd used my telekinesis to knock the Imperium soldiers away so he and Vesper could finally reach each other and trigger their truebond. How I'd let him cut me with his stormsword to hobble me. How I'd deliberately confused and slowed the soldiers' pursuit to give him and Vesper enough time to reach the docking bay where his ship was located.

No, Kyrion might not have put all those pieces together, but he would have his suspicions about my actions that night. I wondered if he'd shared his suspicions with Vesper. Probably not, given the anger and disgust pinching her face.

"Why do you want to kill Kyrion so badly?" Vesper asked. "Because we escaped from Crownpoint? Because you haven't found us and dragged us back to Holloway yet?"

"That's one of many reasons. Kyrion and I despised each other long before you came along. Let's talk about something more interesting. How did you get here?" I asked, genuinely curious. "Why now?"

She chewed on her lower lip. "I'm not sure. I was tinkering with a few projects when I got an alert about the Techwave attack. I started watching the gossipcasts. Great press conference, by the way. Very reassuring."

I uncrossed my arms and held my hands out wide. "What can I say? Command looks good on me. Especially being head of the Arrows. Much better than it ever looked on Kyrion."

She ignored my insults. "Anyway, I watched the gossipcasts for a while. I must have fallen asleep, because I started dreaming about my mindscape. Suddenly, a door appeared, showing me your library. I went over to the door in my mindscape and sort of . . . walked through it. And now here I am, talking to you, whether I want to be or not." She muttered the last few words.

"That sounds rather sketchy, even for space magic."

Vesper slapped her hands on her hips and glared at me.

"It sounds like you can't fully control your seer magic. That's a serious problem," I said in a thoughtful voice. "Especially since Holloway has sicced the Arrows on you, along with every bounty hunter in the Archipelago Galaxy. You and Kyrion are going to need all your truebonded power to stay alive. If I were you, I'd start figuring it out."

Vesper harrumphed. "Why would you want us to do that? I've seen the gossipcasts where you have vowed to bring Kyrion and me to justice for daring to escape Holloway."

I shrugged. "Just following orders. Ask Kyrion. He's done just as many horrific things as I have on Holloway's command."

"You're really going to hunt me down? Your own sister?" Vesper huffed. "I should have known you would be just as awful as Nerezza."

I remembered what she had said during the midnight ball. "Did Nerezza really call you a useless child because you didn't have enough psion power for her liking?"

A shadow passed over Vesper's face, and her pain twinged my telempathy, as sharp as a stormsword stabbing into my chest.

She spun away from me and continued her exploration of the library. Eventually, she wound up at the opposite end of the table where the Quill Corp brewmaker was. She stabbed her finger at the appliance. "Why do you have one of these?"

"Because it's a marvelous device. So is the beverage chiller.

You truly are a mechanical genius. I suppose you get that from our father."

Vesper stared at the brewmaker, a muscle ticking in her clenched jaw.

I pushed away from the table and straightened up. "We didn't get off to a very good start, did we? Perhaps things would be different now if we had."

She spun around to me. "*Good start?* You insulted me, and I burned your clothes. Not to mention us mutually threatening each other at one of the Regal balls."

I winced, thinking back to all the insults I'd hurled her way over the past few months. "I'm sorry I called you a conquest."

She arched an eyebrow. "Would you be sorry if you didn't know I was your sister?"

"I would be less sorry."

Her eyebrow arched a little higher.

"Okay, fine, I wouldn't be sorry at all."

She huffed. "Somehow I doubt Zane Zimmer is ever sorry about anything."

"Someone recently told me that referring to myself in the third person is exceedingly arrogant." I grinned. "But I rather like it when you do it, sis."

"*Do not* call me that." Vesper growled out the words.

She took a step forward, and her fingers twitched, as though she wanted to lunge forward and strangle me. Could she do that in this astral form? Could she touch, move, or affect anything in the physical world? I made a mental note to start researching seer magic. It would be handy to know exactly what tricks my little sister was capable of.

"You might not like our familial connection, but it changes things."

It changes everything. The words rippled through my mind, but I held my tongue. I doubted Vesper was ready to hear my thoughts on the matter, especially since I was still sorting them out for myself.

Vesper shook her head. "Now you sound like Kyrion."

Perhaps I should give Kyrion more credit, if he'd tried to talk to Vesper about what being a Zimmer—my sister—truly meant.

"But *I* know the *truth*," Vesper continued, her eyes glittering with anger. "Our so-called connection changes *nothing*. The Zimmer family has spent the last thirty-seven years pretending I don't exist, and I am quite happy to keep that tradition going by pretending you all don't exist."

I thought of my father's distress when he believed that I was going to hurt Vesper. He might not know his daughter, but he already cared about her. And so did I, as strange as that seemed.

"That was my grandmother's doing. Beatrice never told Wendell anything about you. Me neither."

"What would you have done if she had?"

"I don't know."

"Well, I do know. Nothing. Absolutely *nothing*," Vesper snarled. "You would have kept my existence an ugly little secret just like your grandmother has all these years."

"What Beatrice did to you was wrong," I said in a soft voice. "That's the truth."

"And it's just as ugly as everything else. I don't need—or want—your fucking *apology*," Vesper snarled again. "Just because we share some DNA doesn't make us *family*."

Even more anger filled her eyes, and disgust blasted off her like steam off a bubbling brewmaker. She was right. Just because we shared some DNA didn't make us a family, but my grandmother had drilled the importance of family into my head since birth. Beatrice had always claimed everything she had ever done—good, bad, and ugly—had been for our family. To protect my father and me, along with my assorted cousins and everyone who worked for and depended on House Zimmer. I didn't believe that anymore, but I couldn't—*wouldn't*—ignore my long-lost sister now just because it would be easier and more convenient to do so.

Unlike Beatrice, I didn't care about the scandal it would cause. I just wanted . . . I just wanted to know more about Vesper. What her childhood had been like. If she'd ever wondered who her father was. If she'd ever dreamed about being part of a family.

If she had ever wanted a sibling as badly as I always had. And not just to help me shoulder the burdens of House Zimmer but to be an ally, a confidante, a bloody trusted *friend*.

I was a Regal lord, the heir to House Zimmer, and now, finally, the head of the Arrows, like I'd always wanted, but none of those things had ever come with friends. I'd thought Julieta Delano had been my friend—my *best* friend—but she had been plotting with Rowena Kent, and she would have let me be killed with Kyrion and the other Arrows when the Techwave had shot our ships out of the sky. Julieta had broken every single bit of care, friendship, and concern that I'd ever had for her, and I hadn't even realized it until she was dead.

Julieta's betrayal had cut much, much deeper than I'd let anyone know, except for Kyrion. We'd had a tense conversation about it a few weeks ago, but I don't think even he realized just how much Julieta had hurt me. How embarrassed I was that I hadn't seen her treachery. How humiliated I was to have put my trust in someone so duplicitous. And especially how bloody *furious* I was that she'd tricked me into thinking that she was my friend, that she actually *cared* about me.

Oh, yes. Julieta had taught me a particularly painful lesson that trust was for fools. Well, I would never be that sort of fool again.

But Kyrion hadn't picked up on any of my misery. Like everyone else, Kyrion thought I was an arrogant idiot with minimal feelings. Despite all the years we'd fought together as Arrows, he had never seen the real me.

Vesper and Asterin were the only ones who had ever seen through my Zane Zimmer persona, and they both despised me. There was some lesson in that, probably about my being a masochistic glutton for punishment, but I didn't have the time, patience, or emotional bandwidth to dissect it right now.

"Tell me where you're hiding," I said, focusing on Vesper again. "Make things easier on Kyrion and yourself."

"Why?" she demanded. "So you can do your Arrow duty and drag us both back to Holloway? Hard pass. Although I can see how the idea would appeal to you. Holloway stuffing me in one of the Crownpoint medical labs would solve all your problems about what to do with me, the sister you never knew about and certainly never wanted."

"Far better for me to find you than one of the other Arrows or some bounty hunter who doesn't care how badly they hurt you as long as they get paid," I countered.

She shrugged. "I'm not worried about the other Arrows or any bounty hunters."

"So you're only worried about me? How flattering."

"That is *not* what I said."

I grinned. "You have your interpretation, and I have mine."

Vesper rolled her eyes skyward as if asking whatever gods or higher powers might be left in the galaxy for the patience to deal with me. Yeah, I got that expression a lot. But the fact it was coming from her delighted me in a way I hadn't thought possible. I'd been wrong before. Vesper wasn't a hard problem to be solved.

Why, having a sister might actually be *fun*.

"How is Kyrion treating you?" I drawled. "Have you finally managed to dislodge the perpetual stick that's shoved up his ass?"

Her forehead crinkled with confusion. "If I didn't know

better, I would say it sounds like you're actually concerned about me." She shook her head, as if flinging off that thought. "But we both know that would be a lie. Zane Zimmer is only concerned about himself."

"You told me once that the only good lies are the ones you actually believe yourself," I said in a soft voice. "And I would say it sounds like you actually *want* me to be concerned about you."

"You really do excel at twisting words around." Her face hardened. "And you can certainly turn on the charm when you want to. I can see why you're such a favorite of the gossipcasts. And shampoo companies. Love the new commercial."

Her sarcasm stung, but she was right. I did charm people, and being the arrogant idiot had its advantages. But right now, it was putting me at a disadvantage. All I wanted was to reach some sort of truce with Vesper, but she wasn't going to believe a word I said. I didn't blame my sister, given what Beatrice had done to her, but I still had to try.

Zane Zimmer never gave up.

"My offer remains," I replied in a smooth voice. "Tell me where you are, or at least where you're going. Make things easier on yourself and especially on Kyrion."

"If you come after us, Kyrion *will* kill you." Her face darkened, and fury flashed in her eyes. "And if you hurt Kyrion, then *I* will kill you."

"You would really kill your own brother for the likes of Kyrion Caldaren?" I shook my head. "That truebond has really screwed up your priorities."

"The truebond has nothing to do with how I feel about Kyrion—or you," she snarled.

"And how *do* you feel about me?" I kept my voice light, but my chest tightened with an odd mixture of dread and the smallest spark of hope.

Some of the fury trickled out of Vesper's face, and her lips puckered in thought. "Out of all the people in the galaxy, I never thought I would have any connection to *you*. But I suppose that's just irony working its magic."

"You didn't answer my question. How do you feel about me?"

Vesper's gaze darted from my face to the scorched hole in my coat to the stormsword dangling from my belt. After a few seconds, she raised her gaze to mine again. The silver flecks in her eyes were more pronounced now, like tiny icebergs floating in her dark blue irises. "I don't feel anything for you, Zane—just like you don't feel anything for me. We are two strangers who happen to share some DNA. Nothing more, nothing less."

Her voice was cold, calm, and steady, but I could have sworn the faintest bit of longing flickered off her, tickling my own heart like a nagging finger. Or perhaps that was just my own emotion. Either way, it hardened my resolve, and I walked over and stopped right in front of her.

Vesper tilted her head up, a wary look on her face. I opened my mouth to tell her that we had far more in common than she thought, including all our conflicted feelings about each other.

Vesper turned her head to the side, and her eyes grew distant, as though she was looking at something far, far away. After a few seconds, she looked at me again.

"Do us both a favor. Don't come after me and Kyrion. Don't make us kill you."

"Ah, but that's the one thing I can't do. Holloway has made it crystal clear that if I don't bring at least one of you back to Corios, then he'll take his wrath out on me, along with my father and my grandmother and the rest of House Zimmer." I held my hands out wide. "So you can see my predicament."

Sadness filled her face, and the emotion tweaked my own heart. "I'll warn you again. If you come after Kyrion and me, we *will* kill you, Zane."

"Perhaps." I grinned. "Or maybe I'll surprise the both of you."

Vesper frowned. Her eyes darkened, and she once again seemed to be looking at something far, far away.

"Vesper?" In the distance, a voice called out. I recognized Kyrion's crisp tone.

Vesper looked back at me. Her image flickered again and started to fade away. Our talk was over, and her astral presence was going back to wherever her physical body was.

I held up a clenched fist, then lifted my fingers one by one. I said five words aloud with the motion, mimicking what Kyrion had done when he'd told me that Vesper was my sister the night of the midnight ball.

Vesper flinched. She stared at me a moment longer, then vanished altogether.

She might be gone, but my words echoed through the library. Five little words, seven simple syllables, twenty-two common letters.

See you soon, little sister.

EPILOGUE

VESPER

"**V**esper?" A hand touched my shoulder, startling me awake.

I sucked in a breath and sat bolt upright. My head snapped left and right, but instead of Zane's cluttered library, I was in a maintenance-room-turned-workshop on board the *Dream World*, Kyrion's blitzer.

"Vesper?"

Kyrion loomed over me, the way he so often did. My gaze traced over his longish black hair, dark blue eyes, and pale skin. He looked the same as always, right down to the Arrow uniform he was wearing, and some of the tension in my chest eased. I was here with him, and not stuck half a galaxy away with Zane.

I blew out a breath and sat back in my chair. "I must have fallen asleep."

"Obviously." Kyrion gave me an amused look, then reached down, took hold of the edge of a piece of plastipaper, and gently peeled it off my cheek.

He tossed the clear reusable paper down onto the table in

front of me, causing the gossipcast still playing over the holo-screen to flicker. On the feed, Zane was holding his hands out wide, calling for silence as he answered one question after another about the latest Techwave attack.

"Vesper?" Kyrion frowned. "What's wrong?"

"I saw Zane," I confessed in a low voice. "Through a door in my mindscape."

A mindscape was the place inside a seer's mind, heart, and body where their magic resided. Each mindscape was unique to its seer, although mine was a round room with arched doors, pale blue flowers, and jeweled sapphsidian eyes set into the dark stone walls.

I recapped accidentally going to Zane's library and our heated conversation. When I finished, Kyrion glowered at the hologram of Zane still hovering over the table.

"He's actually going to follow Holloway's orders and come after us? Arrogant bastard." Kyrion spat out the words. "After I told him about you, I thought . . ."

"What?"

Kyrion shrugged his broad shoulders. "That Zane might do the right thing for once in his miserable life. But it looks like I was wrong, and you were right. Your being his sister isn't going to change anything for him. Still, back at Crownpoint, I almost thought . . ." His voice trailed off, and a contemplative look creased his face.

"What?"

"That Zane was helping us escape."

"*Helping* us?" I barked out a laugh. "You almost cut his blasted leg off!"

Kyrion shrugged again. "I did, but I've been thinking about my fight with Zane ever since that night, and something about it just doesn't add up. If I didn't know better, I would almost think that . . ."

"What?" I asked in a wary voice.

Kyrion stared down at me. "That Zane let me cut him on purpose. So he would be too wounded to capture us."

An unexpected bit of hope flared in my stomach, streaking up through my chest like a rocket zipping through the atmosphere, but I swatted it aside before it could crash into my heart. "*No.*" I shook my head. "Zane would *never* do anything to risk his position as the new head of the Arrows. Especially not something as foolish as helping us escape from Holloway."

But even as I said the words, a tiny needle of doubt pricked my heart. I wanted to believe it was true. I wanted to believe Zane had helped us, that he had some small concern and consideration for me, that he might actually view me as his sister.

That one day, I might finally have the loving family I'd always wanted.

But once again, I swatted aside that foolish hope. I'd learned my lesson with Nerezza the hard way when she had abandoned me as a child. Just because you were related to someone didn't make them your *family*. Nerezza had never cared about me, so why would Zane or the rest of the Zimmers?

"Forget about Zane," Kyrion said in a gentle voice. "Have you made any progress on the information Asterin sent you?"

Tivona and Leandra had posted all the details of the solstice celebration attack on the private, encrypted group channel that Daichi had set up for us. Asterin had chimed in with her thoughts and shared the schematics for Jorge Rojillo's new temperature-shielding device, although she hadn't revealed how she had gotten the information. She also hadn't revealed how she'd broken into Jorge's R&D lab or what tech she'd been after, but I didn't begrudge my friend her secrets.

The stars knew I had enough ugly secrets of my own to worry about right now.

I glanced down at the plastipapers that covered the table. "I was looking at the schematics when I fell asleep. Lord Jorge's device seems promising, but I'm not sure what the Techwave wants with climate-control technology. Maybe they think it will keep their new hand cannons from overheating."

"Perhaps," Kyrion agreed. "Or perhaps they've shifted their focus to something else, now that Harkin Ocnus is dead."

"Or maybe General Ocnus is planning something even worse, now that his son is dead," I muttered.

Kyrion and I fell silent, contemplating that horrible possibility.

"Well, whatever the Techwave is up to, it can wait until you get some sleep. Why don't you come back to bed?" Kyrion asked, a husky promise in his voice.

He stepped forward and trailed his fingers down the curve of my spine. Equal parts heat and anticipation spiked through my body at his light touch. "Give me a few minutes to shut everything down."

Kyrion caressed my spine a moment longer, then left the workshop. I slid my chair back from the table and gathered up the loose plastipapers that featured Jorge Rojillo's design schematics, as well as some of my own inventions. I tried to put the papers in order, but after a minute, I gave up and just shoved them all off to the side of the table, creating a haphazard pile. Maybe Zane was right. Maybe clutter did run in our family.

Our family.

My gaze skipped back over to the gossipcast that was still playing over the table. Zane continued to smile at the cameras, but my seer magic surged up, and suddenly, I was seeing a second Zane hovering in the air—my brother as he'd been in his library.

Instead of the cocky, composed, arrogant Arrow I was used to dealing with, Zane had been disheveled, exhausted, and almost heartsick, as though the Techwave attack had bothered him far more than he'd let on in front of the gossipcasters.

His raw vulnerability had surprised me.

So had our conversation.

We'd exchanged barbs and insults, just as we had all the

other times we'd talked to each other over the past few months, and Zane had been smug and infuriating, as usual—until he'd said what Beatrice had done to me was wrong.

He'd seemed so blasted *sincere* in that moment, as if his grandmother's actions and all the secrets she'd kept had truly pained him. But even more surprising had been the way he'd looked at me, as if I were some marvelous creature that he had never encountered before.

I'd expected Zane to sneer at me, dismiss me as wholly unimportant and completely beneath his lofty notice, but I'd had his full, undivided attention, as though our familial connection had been weighing on him as heavily as it had been weighing on me.

And then he'd gone and ruined things by saying that Kyrion and I should turn ourselves in and surrender to him. Arrogant jackass.

I sliced my hand over the holoscreen. The gossipcast vanished, as did the image of the second, more vulnerable Zane that my seer magic had conjured up. I glared at the empty air a moment, then spun away from the table, slapped off the lights, and shut the workshop door behind me.

I strode down the corridor, heading toward a set of tight spiral stairs that would take me to the upper deck where Kyrion was waiting, but I couldn't escape my troubled thoughts, and I kept replaying my conversation with Zane in my mind. His last words haunted me, especially since I couldn't tell whether they had been a threat, a promise, or both.

See you soon, little sister, Zane's voice whispered through my mind.

A sharp finger of unease jabbed into my heart. My long-lost big brother was going to be a problem. I just couldn't see how much of one yet.

Want to know more about Zane Zimmer?
Keep reading for a look at some bonus/deleted
chapters from *Only Good Enemies*, book 2 in the
Galactic Bonds science-fiction fantasy series.

ONE

ZANE

This takes place after Chapter 9 in *Only Good Enemies*.

Holloway droned on for a few more minutes, basically saying the same thing a bunch of different ways: that we were to infiltrate this second suspected Techwave facility, download all the data we could find, kill everyone inside, and destroy it. I stifled a yawn. The Imperium leader certainly loved the sound of his own voice.

A servant sidled up and whispered something in his ear. Holloway nodded, and the servant retreated. He sliced his hand over the table. The facility images vanished, replaced by the ones of Vesper's kidnapping.

"Forget everything I just said. There is no second Techwave facility. I want the three of you to follow Kyrion to Magma 3."

Surprise flickered through me. "Why?"

Holloway ignored my question and turned to Adria. "You've seen Kyrion now. What do you think?"

Adria stared at the doors where Kyrion had exited, a

thoughtful look on her face. "It's hard to tell. He could be bonded to Vesper Quill—or not. I would have to see the two of them together to know for certain."

Shock zinged through my chest like a blaster bolt. "You think Kyrion and Vesper have a *truebond*?"

Even as I said the words, a little voice deep inside me whispered they were true. I was no seer, so I didn't have visions of the future like Julieta Delano had had, but sometimes an odd sense of certainty swept over me, and I simply *knew* things were true, even if no one believed me and there were mountains of evidence to the contrary. And right now, every bit of my psion power was screaming that this was one of those times.

Plus, Kyrion and Vesper having a truebond would explain so many things, including why he kept insisting that he had killed Julieta when I knew that Vesper was the one who had done the deed. If people—if Holloway—knew the truth, they would wonder how Vesper had managed to take down a highly trained Arrow like Julieta, the same way I had been wondering about it for months now. But the truebond must have helped Vesper, must have let her tap into just enough of Kyrion's fighting skills to defeat Julieta.

Grudging admiration filled me. Keeping a secret like that was no easy task. Just when I thought I had Vesper Quill figured out, something entirely unexpected about her surprised me yet again.

"Of course I think they have a bloody truebond," Holloway answered me in a distracted voice. "Why else would I go to so much trouble for a commoner?"

"But there wasn't any sign of it during the ball a few months ago." I gestured toward the spot where the two of them had stood during the truebond test. "Kyrion sliced himself to pieces, but no marks appeared on Vesper's hand."

Holloway let out a merry, mocking chuckle and clapped me on the shoulder. "Oh, Zane, my boy. Sometimes I forget how simple you are, how you always fail to see the big picture."

I kept my pleasant smile fixed in place, but rage curled around my heart like a Tropics dragon wanting to spew fire and burn everything to ash. I might be the heir to House Zimmer, but most people considered me nothing more than a handsome face planted atop a chiseled body. Most of the time, the pigeonholing didn't bother me, and I did nothing to dissuade them from the notion. With someone like Callus Holloway, it was far better to be seen as less than what you actually were. But right now his casual dismissal rankled me in a way it never had before.

"You think Kyrion and Vesper Quill somehow beat your truebond test?" Dargan asked.

"Yes. I know Kyrion better than anyone else. He *never* would have questioned an order before he met Vesper Quill, and the only reason he would hesitate to kill her now was if his own fate was tied to hers." Holloway held his hands out wide. "Like if there was a truebond between them."

I thought back, trying to recall everything I could about the truebond test. Kyrion cutting his hand time and time again, Vesper flinching with every vicious slash, then peeling off her gloves and revealing her unblemished hands.

"I've reviewed the test footage," Adria said. "Kyrion cut his hand. There was no way he could have faked that."

"I agree. Blood *was* pouring out of his hand. I could see it, smell it, taste it in the air. Kyrion didn't fake it, which means Vesper Quill is the one who tricked me." Holloway's eyes glittered with anger. "The little gutter rat is going to pay for that, for keeping me from what is rightfully *mine*. I haven't invested all this time and energy in Kyrion to let him *or* a truebond slip through my fingers."

Despite the gossipcasts presenting it as a romantic ideal, all the Regals knew Holloway was obsessed with truebonds and that he would do *anything* to get his hands on another truebonded pair like Chauncey and Desdemona Caldaren. The gossipcasts might have reported that Desdemona died from a sudden illness, but my grandmother Beatrice had discovered the ugly truth through her network of spies—that Holloway had taken too much of Desdemona's psion power at once and had essentially killed her.

I had only been a boy back then, roughly the same age as Kyrion, but I'd heard my grandmother and my father, Wendell, whispering about the Caldarens. How Chauncey had gone mad with grief and attacked his own son, forcing Kyrion to kill his father in self-defense.

I'd never given much thought to truebonds beyond tuning out the starry-eyed stories on the gossipcasts about how utterly wonderful they must be. But right now, the greed and hunger on Holloway's face made me uneasy. Kyrion and I might be Regal rivals, and I would happily shove my stormsword into his gut given the right opportunity, but even he didn't deserve to endure the misery that Holloway wanted to inflict on him. My gaze strayed back to the images floating over the table. And neither did Vesper Quill.

This was the problem with having a bloody conscience among the Regals and especially among the Arrows. From time to time, it made me want to *help* people, even those I considered bitter enemies. Kyrion had been a thorn in my side for years, and I would never be the leader of the Arrows as long as he was around. On the bright side, Kyrion having a truebond with Vesper meant no more Arrow missions for him. Holloway wouldn't let either one of them out of his sight, not until he had completely broken them.

Adria stared at the image of an unconscious Vesper. "Every truebond is different, so even if Kyrion is bonded to Vesper, it would have a different feel from my connection to Dargan. Especially if they have genuine romantic feelings for each other."

Kyrion Caldaren in love? Before this morning, I would have cackled with disbelief at the absurd idea. My hand crept up to my nose. A good wrench and a skinbond injector from the House Zimmer medic had fixed the damage, but I remembered the frosty rage that had spread across Kyrion's face when I'd insulted Vesper in the training ring. I ran my mouth all the time, and I'd just been trying to distract him and win our sparring match, but he had reacted far more violently than usual. Now I knew why.

Dargan swaggered over and draped his arm across his sister's shoulder. "Wouldn't it be interesting if they *did* have a truebond? Just think of how much fun we could have with them."

An answering smile spread across Adria's face. Images flickered off her and filled my mind. Dargan swiping his sword across Kyrion's side, hobbling him. Adria doing the same thing to Vesper. Kyrion and Vesper on the throne room floor, crawling toward each other, desperately trying to reach the other person however they could . . .

I blinked, and the images vanished. Sometimes I hated the telempathic abilities that came along with being a psion. I could happily have gone the rest of my life without that disturbing glimpse into Adria Byrne's psyche.

"And that is precisely why Zane is going with the two of you," Holloway said in a cold voice. "To ensure that you don't have too much *fun*. Forget what I said earlier about playing with Vesper Quill. I was just trying to provoke a reaction from Kyrion. I want both him and Vesper intact. I can't siphon their magic if they're both on death's doorstep. Is that understood?"

Dargan rolled his eyes, but Adria tilted her head in agreement.

More unease filled me. I was a strong telekinetic and a battle-hardened warrior, but even I was wary of the Byrnes. Their truebond turned the siblings from dangerous to deadly.

If they decided to ignore Holloway's orders and have some *fun* with Kyrion and Vesper after all, then I would be hard-pressed to stop them.

"What are your real orders?" I asked.

"Follow Kyrion to Magma 3," Holloway replied. "Make sure he kills the Techwavers on-site and collects as much information about their plans as possible. Then, when you approach him, find a way to separate him from Vesper Quill."

"What do you want us to do with the woman?" Adria said.

Another cruel grin spread across Holloway's face. "Bring her to me."

He stared at the image of Vesper, even more hunger, greed, and lust surging off him than before. I had always known that Callus Holloway was a villain through and through, but for the first time, I realized the depths of his depravity when it came to truebonds and using the people involved in them. I had never considered myself to be a particularly good person, and I excelled at compartmentalizing the many questionable things I did as an Arrow, but this twinged my conscience in a way that nothing had in a long time. I wasn't quite sure why.

Dargan frowned. "But you need both Vesper *and* Kyrion to have the full power of a truebonded pair. So what do you want us to do about Kyrion?"

"Yes," Adria chimed in. "If they really are bonded, he won't let us just take Vesper away. He'll do everything in his power to hang on to her."

Holloway shrugged. "Then fight him. That's why I summoned you both. You two are the only Arrows and psions strong enough to take on Kyrion and live." He waved his hand at me again. "While Kyrion is distracted, Zane can get Vesper onto a ship and off-planet. He shouldn't have nearly as many problems with her as the two of you will have with Kyrion."

An image of Julieta's bloody body slumped in the Kent Corp weapons lab flashed through my mind. I seemed to be the only one who realized that Vesper had killed the other Arrow—and just how smart and powerful she was.

My gaze flicked from Holloway to Adria to Dargan. All of them were cruel, sly, and dangerous in their own ways, as were Kyrion and Vesper. This was a situation that could swiftly spin out of control and end up costing several people their lives.

I was okay with that, as long as mine wasn't one of the lives lost.

"You're giving us permission to engage with Kyrion? Finally!" Dargan cracked his knuckles. "That arrogant bastard thinks he's untouchable, and I'm going to enjoy showing him just how wrong he is."

Holloway held up a warning finger. "You can bend Kyrion, but don't break him. Let him escape, if you must, but I want him alive and functioning. As long as I have Vesper Quill, Kyrion will come after her sooner or later, and then I will have them *both*, along with their combined power. With their truebond, I can finally eliminate the Techwave once and for all, along with the Regals who are secretly aligned with the group and plotting against me."

Dargan and Adria murmured their agreement. I chimed in as well, even though the words tasted like poison in my mouth, and another uncomfortable twinge rippled through my body.

For the first time in a long, long time, I actually felt sorry for Kyrion Caldaren.

Holloway gave us a few more orders, then dismissed us. Adria, Dargan, and I got into an elevator, rode down to the armory level, and split up to grab some supplies. I made sure the siblings were busy, then ducked into a bathroom, locked the door, and turned on the water in one of the sinks. I wet my hands and ran them through my hair, mussing it up just a bit, as though I was in here washing up before we left for Magma 3.

I left the water running while I dried off my hands. Then I flipped one of the zippers on my Arrow jacket around so it was upside down. A faint hum emanated, and an electrical charge filled the air around me, one that would scramble any nearby cameras and listening devices. The zipper was one of my father's many inventions. House Zimmer had produced some excellent spies over the years, myself included, and Wendell's job was to create all the equipment we needed to keep tabs on our enemies and allies and maintain House Zimmer's exalted position among the Regals. Something that was more important than ever, given the increasing hostilities with the Techwave.

When I was certain no one could see or hear me, I pulled my tablet out of my pocket and swiped through to the appropriate screen. A moment later, a woman's face appeared. She was in her eighties, and her silver hair had been teased out into a fluffy oval around her head. Her skin was rosy, but her eyes were the same pale, cold blue as mine.

Beatrice Zimmer, my grandmother and the head of House Zimmer, sat back in her chair, a cup of tea steaming in her hand. "Well? What are your orders? Are you going after the Techwave again?"

"Something like that. Although Holloway has a far more valuable prize in mind."

I told her everything that had happened in the throne room, including Holloway sending Kyrion off to rescue Vesper, even as he sent Adria, Dargan, and me along in their wake to subdue and deliver the two of them back to Crownpoint.

"So Kyrion finally formed a truebond with someone," Beatrice murmured. "It doesn't surprise me. His parents had one of the strongest bonds I've ever seen. Even after the true-bond test a few months ago, I suspected that something was going on. I've sensed a . . . shift in him recently."

My grandmother was a very strong telempath, able to pick

up on people's thoughts and feelings from great distances, like a spider sitting in a web of emotions.

"What do you want me to do?" I asked. "Kyrion is no friend of mine. Neither is Vesper Quill."

My grandmother's lips puckered in thought. "What do *you* think you should do, darling?"

I bit back an annoyed huff. Beatrice was always turning things around, always trying to get me to forge my own path instead of following her orders. She claimed it was part of my training to take over House Zimmer one day. Normally, I didn't mind the prodding, but right now it annoyed me.

Sometimes it was nice to be told to just kill someone and be done with things.

"What do you want me to do about Kyrion and Vesper?" I repeated.

Beatrice sucked in a breath as if to say something. But then she stopped and shook her head, as if dismissing the thought, whatever it was. "Do whatever you think is best, darling. I trust you."

Normally, her vote of confidence would have pleased me, but I couldn't shake the suspicion that she knew far more about the situation than she was letting on.

"Regardless of how things play out, it's a shame you're leaving so soon," Beatrice continued. "I'm having lunch with Lady Asterin before she departs from Corios later today. I'd hoped the two of you might meet again, but that won't happen now." Her head tilted to the side, and her lips puckered again. "Although you'll see her again soon enough."

My eyes narrowed. "What does that mean? Are you having some psionic vision of the future? Or just imagining your next scheme coming to fruition?"

Beatrice smiled and took a sip of tea, which was her preferred method of not answering questions, along with looking at people until they either dropped their gaze from her steady, intimidating stare or stammered out exactly what she wanted to know.

Despite my annoyance with my grandmother's lack of information, I was glad that I was leaving on a mission and wouldn't have to meet with Asterin again.

Lady Asterin Armas was a member of Erzton society, and her mother and stepfather, Verona and Aldrich Collier, were among the leaders of the powerful rival group. The Erztonians controlled many of the minerals in the Archipelago Galaxy, and Asterin herself owned some Frozon moons that were rumored to be rich in lunarium deposits.

Holloway had brought Lady Asterin to Corios and introduced her to Kyrion at the spring ball, hoping the two of them might spark a truebond. But if what Holloway said was true, then Kyrion had already been bonded to Vesper before he had even met Asterin.

Either way, nothing had happened between Kyrion and Asterin, so her handler had set his sights on another Regal lord: me. Over the past few months, Asterin had visited Corios several times, and we'd been forced together at one society event after another. Every interaction between us had been genteel and polite and had made me grind my teeth in frustration.

Asterin Armas was a beautiful puzzle I couldn't quite decipher. Beatrice and Wendell thought she was exactly what she appeared to be—a lovely noble lady with perfect manners—but I thought Asterin had hidden facets, just like the lunarium she mined on all those Frozon moons.

A loud banging sounded, and the bathroom door shuddered in its frame. "Let's go, pretty boy!" Dargan's annoyed voice barked out.

I glanced back down at my tablet. "Gotta jet."

"Be careful, darling," Beatrice said.

I winked at her. "Aren't I always?"

That teased a laugh out of her. "Never."

I slid my tablet into my pocket and flipped the zipper on my jacket back into its normal position, releasing the electrical countersurveillance field. Then I unlocked the door and jerked it open.

Dargan wasn't expecting the motion, and he almost toppled over. I put my hand on his shoulder and shoved him away. I was a strong telekinetic, so I put a little psion power into the blow, sending him staggering all the way back across the hallway. Dargan bounced off the opposite wall and skidded to a stop.

"Hey! You did that on purpose," he accused.

"Absolutely," I replied in a light, cheery voice. "Pushing you around is one of my favorite pastimes—and so surprisingly easy."

Anger stained his cheeks a bright red. His hands clenched into fists, and telekinetic power rippled off him in dangerous waves, making the bathroom door behind me *creak* back and forth in warning.

"Easy, Dargan," I drawled. "You wouldn't want to start a fight you can't finish."

His hand dropped to his stormsword, and I could see the calculations going on behind his eyes as he debated whether he could kill me by himself. The answer was no, and we both knew it. Oh, Dargan was a formidable fighter, but it was his truebond with Adria that gave him an advantage over me, not his own psionic skills and strength.

Footsteps sounded, and Adria stopped between the two of us. "What is taking you two so bloody long?"

Dargan jerked his chin at me. "Ask the pretty boy. He's the one who locked himself in the bathroom."

Adria's gaze swung around to me, suspicion flaring in her eyes. "Why is that?"

I gestured at my still-damp hair. "This doesn't happen by

accident, you know. It takes serious effort to look this good. Besides, some gossipcast reporters might be hanging around the palace, and I want to give them a show before we leave."

I ran my fingers through my blond hair, fussily arranging the thick locks just so. Dargan and Adria rolled their eyes, dismissing me and my vanity just as I wanted them to, just as everyone always did.

"Let's go," Adria said, striding past me. "According to Holloway's spies, Kyrion has already left Corios. We can't afford to get too far behind him. Holloway might think this will be an easy mission, but I know better."

"How so?" I asked, falling into step beside her, still playing the part of the nonchalant idiot.

"Because nothing in the galaxy is more dangerous than a truebonded pair. Whether he realizes it or not, Kyrion will do anything to protect Vesper Quill, and vice versa."

"Just as you and Dargan would do anything to protect each other?" I asked, genuinely curious.

"Of course," Adria replied.

"Aw, don't worry, sis." Dargan jogged up and draped his arm across her shoulder. "No one is stronger than we are together. We'll make short work of Kyrion, and Vesper too, if she tries to cross us."

Once again, the image of a bloody, injured Kyrion and Vesper crawling toward each other on the throne room floor flashed through my mind. I was no seer, but I couldn't help but think it was a portent of things to come—for all of us.

BONUS CHAPTER
TWO

ZANE

This takes place after Chapter 14 in *Only Good Enemies*.

"He's not bloody here!" Dargan growled, swinging his sword back and forth in an annoyed motion. Adria glanced up at the ship. "Judging from the lack of psionic echoes, Kyrion was never on this blitzer."

The three of us had arrived on Magma 3 about thirty minutes ago to find the Techwave facility engulfed in flames. With no one to control them, a few Black Scarabs had been aimlessly wandering around, but Adria, Dargan, and I had made quick work of them. If there had been any human survivors, they'd had the good sense to flee from the fire or hide at the sight of three Arrows slicing heads off suits of armor.

After we'd finished with the Scarabs, we'd started searching for Kyrion, and a scan of the surrounding area had revealed this blitzer, Kyrion's official Imperium ship, sitting in a field about half a mile away from the Techwave facility.

No energy shields or defensive measures had been activated

around the ship, so Dargan had used his enhanced strength to forcibly lower the cargo bay ramp. Then he and Adria had rushed on board, stormswords in hand, ready to attack Kyrion the moment they spotted him.

I had followed at a more leisurely pace. I might dislike Kyrion, but he was an excellent warrior, and I had no desire to get cut down for Holloway's greed. Better to let the Byrnes bear the brunt of Kyrion's fury. Then I could come in and deal with the bloody mess of whomever was still alive.

But Kyrion hadn't been on board the blitzer, and there had been no sign of Vesper Quill either. Kyrion wasn't as blindly loyal to Holloway as I'd thought. Or perhaps he had seen through Holloway's ruse. Either way, the Arrow wasn't here, although he had left some interesting toys behind, including a spy camera.

The camera had been attached to the flight controls, looking like just another little black navigation box, but I'd recognized the House Zimmer tech for what it truly was, and I'd plucked it out of the row of similar boxes. A tiny light on the side burned blue, indicating that the camera was recording, so I'd picked up and grinned into the lens.

"Clever, Kyrion," I murmured. "Using House Zimmer tech to spy on your own ship. Very clever."

Then I'd left the blitzer and rejoined the Byrnes. I hadn't told Dargan and Adria about the camera, though—or the fact that it was currently recording us.

Dargan stabbed his sword at the still-burning Techwave facility in the distance. "Maybe one of the Techies zapped him. Maybe he's already toast inside the factory."

I laughed. "Your naïveté is almost charming. Kyrion Caldaren is much too stubborn to be killed in anything as clean, simple, and easy as a factory explosion."

Adria nodded. "Zane is right. Kyrion's not dead in the factory, which means he left on another ship, most likely with Vesper Quill."

She shoved her sword onto her belt. Then she wet her lips, stepped forward, and held her hands out, skimming her palms back and forth, almost as if she was tasting the air with her fingertips. Psion power ebbed and flowed around her, surging back and forth with her slow, steady movements.

"Oh, yes," she purred. "Kyrion and Vesper left together, and the truebond between them is stronger than ever."

Dargan stepped up beside her and sniffed the air as though he was trying to catch a hint of a Regal lady's perfume. "Oh, yeah. Holloway was right. Kyrion and Vesper are *definitely* bonded. It smells all sweet and gooey, like a marshmallow, but with burned edges. Definitely a romantic bond. It's going to be *so* much fun for us."

Matching grins spread across their faces. The sister and brother started laughing, their chuckles ringing out like a dark, ominous chorus. Suddenly, I was very glad that I wasn't Kyrion Caldaren.

"Where do you think Kyrion and Vesper went?" I asked, kicking one of the shiny black rocks that were strewn across the ash-covered field. "We have to find them. Holloway is already pissed that they beat his truebond test. He'll be even more pissed if we don't deliver them as promised."

Adria shrugged. "Holloway had a spy in the Techwave facility. Maybe they got out before it exploded and they know where Kyrion and Vesper are heading."

She yanked her tablet out of her pocket, stalked away a few feet, and started typing on the device.

I had nestled the spy camera in a pocket on the front of my Arrow jacket so that the device was pointing out toward everything that was in front of me. I reached up and pretended to fiddle with a button while I checked the camera. The small blue light was on, indicating that it was still recording and transmitting.

I turned to Dargan. "Why will Vesper and Kyrion's bond be fun for you and Adria?"

A grin spread across Dargan's face. "What did you think I meant?"

"Nothing good."

His grin widened. "Exactly! I've always hated Kyrion. Such a bloody arrogant dick. Always bossing all the Arrows around, even though Adria and I are much more powerful than he's ever *dreamed* of being. Kyrion thinks because he's Holloway's little pet project that he's untouchable, but I'm going to enjoy showing him otherwise."

Dargan stroked his finger along the edge of his sword like it was a housecat he was petting. "While you were off getting pretty for the mission, Holloway summoned Adria and me back to the throne room for a few final instructions. He told us that we can have a little fun with Kyrion and Vesper before he sticks them in one of the palace labs and siphons off their magic. Holloway isn't going to screw around with them for years like he did with Kyrion's parents. He's planning to take all their magic at once."

My stomach clenched. "But that will kill them."

Dargan clapped me on the back. "That's the idea."

Kyrion and I had always been rivals, even when we were just boys fighting for the same academy awards and accolades, and I had never liked him. But I had been in Holloway's labs, and I'd seen the horrific experiments his scientists conducted on anyone who displeased the Imperium ruler. Killing your enemies was one thing; torturing them for sport was another. Callus Holloway truly was a cold, cruel, conniving bastard. Me too, but there were some lines that I wouldn't cross—and torture for torture's sake was one of them.

"And what do you and Adria get out of this arrangement?" I asked, genuinely curious but also dreading the answer.

"People think Callus Holloway is the only one who can tap into a truebond," Dargan replied. "But if you're part of a truebonded pair, then you can feel the power of other bonded pairs around you, just like Adria and I could taste and smell Kyrion and Vesper's connection."

He glanced over at Adria, but she was still typing on her tablet, so he leaned closer to me. "Holloway doesn't report every truebond, and the other Regals have no idea how many couples he's drained over the years. Whenever Adria and I come across a truebonded pair, we take some of their energy for ourselves before we turn them over to Holloway. It's like sinking your teeth into a juicy steak. The taste just explodes on your tongue, and it fills you up with more power than you ever imagined."

Dargan's gray eyes gleamed with anticipation, and he lifted his fingers to his mouth and blew a chef's kiss. Once again, my stomach clenched, with dread or perhaps a touch of guilt.

Adria finished with her tablet and came back over to us. "According to Holloway's spy, Kyrion and Vesper are most likely headed to Tropics 33. The Techwave is planning something there, and the two of them have probably decided to be brave, noble heroes and try to stop it."

Dargan snorted. "Idiots."

Adria nodded in agreement. "Idiots indeed. New orders. Holloway wants us to let Kyrion and Vesper stop whatever the Techwave is doing. Then we'll move in and capture them."

Dargan and Adria headed for my ship, but my fingers crept up to the spy camera still hidden in my jacket pocket. I could turn it off—I *should* turn it off. Kyrion, or, more likely, his chief of staff, Daichi Hirano, was probably reviewing the footage right now. I would have been if our positions had been reversed.

But I couldn't do that. Not yet.

I pulled the camera out of my pocket and flipped it around so that I was once again staring into the lens. I kept my face carefully blank, although disgust continued to churn in my stomach, along with a tiny bit of regret. As an Arrow, I'd done a lot of questionable things on Holloway's orders, but this assignment . . . *bothered* me in a way that nothing had in a long, long time. I still wasn't quite sure why.

"See you soon, Kyrion." I winked at the camera, once again playing the part of the arrogant idiot. "You too, Vesper."

My hand covered the lens, and I finally turned off the device. If nothing else, I'd given Kyrion a clear warning that we were heading his way. So why did I still feel so shitty about things?

"Zane!" Dargan yelled at me from the top of the cargo bay ramp on my blitzer. "Stop mooning into space. Let's go!"

I slid the camera back into my pocket and ambled toward the ship. My boots scuffed through more of the shiny black rocks, which crunched like broken glass. I grimaced and quickened my pace, but each one of my heavy steps seemed as loud as an alarm blaring out all my disgust, guilt, and regret.

I truly had picked a terrible time to grow a conscience.

Thank you for reading *Only Hard Problems*.
Zane, Vesper, and Kyrion will return
in another **Galactic Bonds** adventure.

ABOUT THE AUTHOR

Jennifer Estep is a *New York Times, USA Today,* and internationally bestselling author who prowls the streets of her imagination in search of her next fantasy idea.

Jennifer is the author of the **Galactic Bonds, Section 47, Elemental Assassin, Crown of Shards, Gargoyle Queen,** and other fantasy series. She has written more than forty-five books, along with numerous novellas and stories.

In her spare time, Jennifer enjoys hanging out with friends and family, doing yoga, and reading fantasy and romance books. She also watches way too much TV and loves all things related to superheroes.

For more information on Jennifer and her books, visit her website at **www.jenniferestep.com** or follow her online on Facebook, Twitter, Instagram, Amazon, BookBub, and Goodreads. You can also sign up for her newsletter: **www.-jenniferestep.com/contact-jennifer/newsletter/**

Happy reading, everyone!

OTHER BOOKS
BY JENNIFER ESTEP

THE GALACTIC BONDS SERIES
Only Bad Options
Only Good Enemies
Only Hard Problems (Zane Zimmer book)

THE SECTION 47 SERIES
A Sense of Danger
Sugar Plum Spies (holiday book)

THE ELEMENTAL ASSASSIN SERIES
FEATURING GIN BLANCO

BOOKS
Spider's Bite
Web of Lies
Venom
Tangled Threads
Spider's Revenge
By a Thread
Widow's Web
Deadly Sting
Heart of Venom
The Spider
Poison Promise
Black Widow
Spider's Trap
Bitter Bite
Unraveled

Snared
Venom in the Veins
Sharpest Sting
Last Strand
Stings and Stones (short story collection)

E-NOVELLAS
Haints and Hobwebs
Thread of Death
Parlor Tricks
Kiss of Venom
Unwanted
Nice Guys Bite
Winter's Web
Heart Stings
Spider and Frost (crossover novella)

THE CROWN OF SHARDS SERIES
Kill the Queen
Protect the Prince
Crush the King

THE GARGOYLE QUEEN SERIES
Capture the Crown
Tear Down the Throne
Conquer the Kingdom

THE BLACK BLADE SERIES
Cold Burn of Magic
Dark Heart of Magic
Bright Blaze of Magic

THE BIGTIME SERIES
Karma Girl
Hot Mama

Jinx
A Karma Girl Christmas (holiday novella)
Nightingale
Fandemic

THE MYTHOS ACADEMY SPINOFF SERIES
FEATURING RORY FORSETI

Spartan Heart
Spartan Promise
Spartan Destiny

THE MYTHOS ACADEMY SERIES
FEATURING GWEN FROST

BOOKS
Touch of Frost
Kiss of Frost
Dark Frost
Crimson Frost
Midnight Frost
Killer Frost

E-NOVELLAS AND SHORT STORIES
First Frost
Halloween Frost
Spartan Frost
Spider and Frost (crossover novella)

OTHER WORKS
The Beauty of Being a Beast (fairy tale)
Write Your Own Cake (worldbuilding essay)

Printed in the USA
CPSIA information can be obtained
at www.ICGtesting.com
LVHW090743250224
772533LV00008B/14